Evil Never Sleeps

Tales of Light and Darkness

ROBERT FLEMING

Manta —

This one was very difficult to write. I hope you enjoy the stories. Take care —

Robert Fleming

First published by Indigo Ink, an imprint of Full Sail
Publishing, Chicago, Illinois 2019

First edition

ISBN: 978-0-9910823-1-5

Editing by Zander Vyne

FULL SAIL PUBLISHING

Contents

Praise for Evil Never Sleeps

"*Evil Never Sleeps* busts open its rib cage and exposes author Robert Fleming's heart beautifully. Jordan Peele should consider this collection for his *Twilight Zone* series! Grim and ghastly, each story bares its teeth—guaranteeing that readers will flinch."

—Rose Caraway, host of *The Kiss Me Quick's Erotica Podcast*

"Reading Robert Fleming's *Evil Never Sleeps* is, yes, a pleasure: his stories bite, his characters live and breathe, his language perfectly flows, there are bottomless depths, his words linger in thoughts and dreams long after the pages have been turned...but there is more than pleasure in reading these wonderfully written stories. Being able to immerse yourself in *Evil Never Sleeps* is an honor: to be able to encounter Fleming's art, his music, his magic, is a gift you will thank yourself, and most of all, the author, for this powerful experience."

—M. Christian, author of many books and stories

"Robert Fleming's stories are intricate portraits of wicked history, brimming with secrets and pulsing with jazz style. Race and class, sex and violence, crime and politics are all explored with a soloist's edge. The stories here range over the course of the twentieth century and up to the present day, creating a patchwork portrait of a dangerous century."

—Thomas Roche, author of *The Panama Laugh*

"Fleming, a writer at his peak, leads his readers down the rabbit hole of human nature. He exposes human frailty, strengths, and loneliness with a depth that allows you to see yourself in the characters. When you emerge on the other side, you are forever changed. Masterfully written."

—Dean Jean-Pierre, author of *The Killer in Me*

"*Evil Never Sleeps: Tales of Light and Darkness* is a collection that exposes Robert Fleming's singular and uninhibited voice. The stories animate the everyday and the spectacular, the surreal and the material: sex, desire, loneliness, violence, intimacy, failure, and wonderment. And Fleming knows something about writing into being the messy and nuanced lives of his characters."

—Darnell L. Moore, author of *No Ashes in the Fire: Coming of Age Black and Free in America*

"If the late jazz legend Sun Ra wrote a book of fiction, it would be like this—ingenious, way-out, probing, daring, mind-altering, leading-edge. Robert Fleming is all refined sensibilities and grim bravado. His abilities and narratives exhilarate and frighten me. They freak me out. They turn me on. They make me ask deep questions. This cat is so baaad!"

—Colin Channer, author of *Waiting in Vain*

"A compelling collection of unsettling tales, evil as a butterfly knife to the throat. Fleming's daring visions resonate long after you've turned the final page."

—Brandon Massey, author of *Dark Corner*

"The belief in a supernatural source of evil is not necessary; men alone are quite capable of every wickedness."
Joseph Conrad

"When choosing between two evils, I always like to try the one I've never tried before."
Mae West

"The end result excuses any evil or mischief."
Fats Waller

Foreword

Reading a collection of short stories by a master of the form is one of the great literary pleasures, especially when the writer treats his work as a set of variations on a powerful theme yet manages to make each story as unique as a snowflake.

I discovered this as a young reader, devouring mythology, horror comic books, and tales from *Arabian Nights.* Looking back, I realize the stories I liked most had strong themes, compelling storytelling, and smart, sophisticated writing that stuck a nerve. The authors provided wildly imaginative glimpses into worlds that seemed far removed from my own. And I could not get enough.

Over the years, my taste has evolved. Yes, I love literary short story writing, but my pulse quickens when I am in the arms of a writer who knows the power of theme. Of surprise. Of creating characters and worlds that introduce me to people and places outside my reality or show me something new about myself or those around me while also entertaining me.

A good writer is like a musician, a pied piper of words who leads you, heart and mind, into places you might not have gone otherwise.

A steady bass beat pulses through Robert Fleming's narratives as he deftly examines the point of our lives and the sometimes sad and uncanny ways in which our fragile hearts, societal norms, and changeable beliefs determine our destinies.

His writing demands readers to think about these things, even as they are lulled with stories ranging from funny to horrifying.

Fleming understands groundbreaking writing might be upsetting. He knows great literature is not polite, doesn't shove uncomfortable things in closets, and doesn't care about your feelings. It only asks that you feel.

Evil Never Sleeps is a daring, sometimes unsettling portrait of the Black experience throughout history that hits on fundamental truths. Linked by strong themes, this is a story collection done right. Some of the stories might make you flinch, but it is hard to look away. The writing burns with raw, elemental power. The characters are complex and compelling, and the writing is sharp and brave. Fleming's dark, captivating imagination shines in this wildly diverse collection that is both gripping and timely.

This collection gives readers compact treasures of emotion and realism often wrapped in a deceptive cloak of normalcy. Though Fleming's stories are worlds unto themselves, each is a grand carnival of the troubling and absurd; the beautiful and the profane blend to form a whole that speaks to the discord and disillusion, hope and triumphs of the Black experience.

Rich with novelistic density, Fleming's stories make *Evil Never Sleeps* a full-fledged feast. Observational and piercing, some of Fleming's stories expose how fraught, and emotionally explosive, our search for connection with other human beings can be. The range of settings, characters, and styles makes for a recurring sense of surprise for the reader.

Evil Never Speaks is a wry, intelligent collection that skillfully navigates the boundary between the demands of faith and the persistence of doubt. In seizing upon the oddities of our shared histories and our enduring, individual searches for meaning,

Fleming finds worthy subjects to illuminate at every turn. Soldiers, musicians, traveling preachers, politicians, religious zealots, the famous, and the ordinary all rub shoulders here, each asking you to sit awhile and listen or to walk in their shoes until you understand them.

Plenty of writers have explored racism and the failings of man. However, Fleming, a writer who feels like the novelist equivalent of filmmakers Spike Lee and Robert Altman, has managed to write stories on the subject that feel fresh. His characters often mess up, in both small and spectacular fashion, but their transgressions often prompt our sympathy, thanks to Fleming's insightful narration. These are tales that make you think, squirm, and sigh with understanding. What more could any reader ask for when immersing themselves in the world of a writer's mind?

Robert Altman said to play it safe is not to play, and if you don't have a leg to stand on, you can't put your foot down. Somehow, I am quite sure Robert Fleming would agree.

Zander Vyne, Editor

That Only Seems Fair: A Preface

Some say the black community does not read short fiction because the form is too much work on the mind. I say that's bull because nothing grabs my imagination like short fiction. I read everything, from James Baldwin's *Going to Meet the Man* (1965), Alice Walker's *In Love and Trouble* (1973), to Langston Hughes's *The Ways of White Folks* (1934), and Hal Bennett's *Insanity Runs In My Family (1977)*.

At first, fictional books of color often captured my attention the most. Then, in junior high school, my Spanish teacher, Wally Mucha, gave me the international-literary bug. He introduced me to writers like Gabriel Garcia Marquez, Jorge Luis Borges, and Jorge Amado. My English teacher also passed on a discarded novel by Kobo Abe.

Later, I discovered other Japanese scribes like Yasunari Kawabata, Haruki Murakami, Yukio Mishima, and Koji Suzuki. They fed my creative soul as I began to try my hand at writing short fiction like those I admired so much.

When I began writing, like a child following a teacher, I wanted to duplicate the old school classics and the bold, global novels, but times have changed. Now, after years of writing and publishing and a life well-lived, my voice is my own.

"Don't be afraid to separate from the pack," advised my friend and literary mentor John A. Williams, author of the ground-breaking *Clifford's Blues* (1999). "Tell the story of our people from all angles—culturally, emotionally, historically, and politically. Avoid the familiar and the cliche. Be bold, adventurous, and provocative."

That's the bar I shoot for, and I hope I've delivered here. This is my second collection of short stories. In some cases, I tried to reclaim the spark and funk of old-school literary bloodlines. I played with light surrealism, colored with my grand passions of politics, music, and history.

I've included some of the work of my alter ego, Cole Riley. Cole was born of a need to keep a roof over my head and food in the icebox, back in the late 1970s. There are some of his better works here.

As a reporter for a New York daily newspaper, my city editor liked to lecture me on the merits of evil and its role in the book of life. He'd rave about the beauty, serenity, righteousness, and correctness of evil. I didn't see it that way. I was raised in the church, on old gospel hymns, and Sunday school. Evil was chaos and mayhem, the dark alchemy, and wickedness caused by seemingly random waves from the withered fingers of some hateful white wizard.

But what do I know? What do any of us know? The best I can do is reflect the world back to readers, to expand on troubling issues and their accompanying confusion. There is some crazy stuff out here, and many folks don't know how to deal with it. Evil is at full strength in our world. And we all know good doesn't always triumph over evil. Evil often trumps common sense or rational thinking and laughs at what's right. These stories deal with some of those issues.

I hope you enjoy them as much as I enjoyed writing them. I hope they are relevant. However, I'll write other things, other than the plagues of slavery, Jim Crow, poverty, and the despair that grips our people. There is much more to our community than hopelessness and violence. We are more than drugged, depressed, deranged souls huddled in the Hood, hurting and killing each other, waiting for the Man to break us off a piece of paradise. We are hopeful. We are full of imagination, fantasy, and creativity. We are resourceful and resilient. And we know we must stand up, be courageous, and deal with this thing called evil, whatever comes.

Robert Fleming
New York City
Spring 2019

Responding to Her Touch

The illness of loneliness is upon him again. His lips sting from the mouthpiece of the trumpet, from long sets at the club, from the bruised kisses of a woman who doesn't belong to him. What is he doing in Paris anyway? He should have kept his black ass in the States instead of wandering around all over the world, instead of seeking something he can't name. Forty years old, broke, no wife, no kids. A nigger without a portfolio.

He pours himself a shot of cognac, heaves a sigh, and places a Fats Navarro record on the phonograph. A memory of Fat Girl blowing the trumpet so sweetly, so soulfully, sweeps through him as the notes rush and circle the room. Fats on *Our Delight*.

Stretching out on the bed again, he pushes the empty liquor bottles and crumpled candy wrappers aside to make room for his long legs. There is something about drinking that makes the time go by softly, easily, without the sudden starts and stops that normally accompany the passage of a day. A little scotch, a nip of gin, a splash of bourbon on ice, or a half belly of *vin rouge*. It all gives his existence a veneer of civilization. Pretties matter a bit. The stocking cap on his shiny conked hair itches.

He thinks of his Congo cutie. Solange. Another man's woman. He replays her arrival two hours earlier, savoring every moment of the memories. She puts down her purse and without a word, takes off her summer dress. She never wears underwear. She opens her purple thighs wide and pulls back the lips of her sex. He looks down into its scarlet throat. She said she smells the white woman on her man's penis when she comes home. Her husband, Jacques, is always out catting. She says the white bitches stink. White woman *basali na masoko na maimai*, she says in her native tongue. He likes his Congo cutie's scent. His sheets smell of her—strongly female, like ripe tropical fruit. Her luminous face is purple against the pillow as she urges him to shove it inside, to be rough, and starts moving her ass against him like crazy while he reaches under to worry her clit with a finger.

Solange says she wants to feel him at the back of her throat, and he stops pumping into her so he can apply his tongue to her breasts, teasing the nipples to hardness, and then to her sex. She is tight down there, narrow, warmer than her mouth, and moist. She raises her ass to him, and he plunges into her very deep, lost in pleasure, but she stops him before they come. She guides him into position above her head. His legs straddles her as he pushes himself into her pillow mouth. Steady thrusts. A hot liquid flows from her bushy cleft onto her strong thighs. He reaches around to dip his fingers into her gushing honey and brings them to his lips. Then, he works his dick into her, riding her bareback, sweat on her face and breasts, until she howls and bites him on the shoulder.

"Jacques doesn't satisfy me," she murmurs to him in almost-precise English. "His thing is too little. But he's a good man otherwise. His friends hate me. His Little Savage, they call me."

"Does Jacques say anything to them about the way they treat

you?" he asks, lighting a cigarette. "He wouldn't let them get away with that if he were any kind of man."

"He is like so many Frenchmen, very arrogant about his culture, art, and aesthetics," she says, reaching for the cigarette. "He will not talk sensibly about anything. He talks to me like a child. You see, Cole, I know I'm not respectable in his eyes."

"Then why don't you leave?"

She folds her arms and rests her head on them. "I don't know. Maybe I can go to the Sorbonne, take classes and improve myself. He says he'd pay for it. But that doesn't change how his women friends look at me. To them, everyone and everything is more civilized than the African. One asked me if I had any pygmies in my family. They watch me all the time when we go to events. They watch me with a hate that is not hidden. They comment rudely on my makeup, my hair, my choice of clothes, and the size of my ass. I have a fat, African ass."

He laughs. "But I love your African ass."

The mirror is in her hands, and she watches herself in it, studying her features intently. "The white women are prettier, more cultured, yes? Jacques tells me all the time there is one way toward civilization, and that road goes through the world of the whites. If that is true, then that is bad, yes?"

"Beauty is in the eye of the beholder, someone said, and I believe that jive." He takes the mirror from her. "It's a shame how their words can brainwash our minds, changing how we look, how we think, what we're worth."

She spins around in a tight circle, nude, her breast flopping. Two horny French sailors across the way hides behind the curtain in their window, getting an eyeful. Unconcerned about them, she continues her strange inspection of herself. "They won't let me be one of them. They accept me only when I play

3

the pagan, the primitive Congo girl." Turning to face him, she asked suddenly, "Cole Riley, why are you here in Paris?"

"I ask myself that all the time." He takes a puff on the cigarette. "America's a hard place to live if you're a black man. Jim Crow lets you know it's for white folks. We can't vote, must sit in special sections in diners and on buses, can't do a lot of things whites can do. After the war, after my brother was lynched in his army uniform in Alabama by some rednecks, I came to Paris and never went back. There's nothing for me there. Not anymore."

She laughs harshly. "The modern civilized man and woman. Jacques fucks my inferiority complex, and I think it's love. Now, I hate it when he touches me. Come here, *Cherie*, make love to me again."

"Do you come with him in you?" He needs some rest.

"Never. But with you, sometimes." She gets up, pours some water into the basin, and scrubs her crotch with soap. She kisses his cheeks, says she'll see him later, and leaves.

In the afternoon, before going to the gig, Cole strolls over to Café Tournon near the Luxembourg Gardens, a center of French life crawling with colored artists and writers. The black bohemian life. He has seen Richard Wright, William Gardner Smith, even that Himes fellow. He digs the colored folks here, especially the writers. They stake him a drink now and then. They are all over the place, in the Latin Quarter, the Left Bank, even down among the Arabs in poor Belleville.

Yet, the differences would sometimes get to him. So far away from home, from his roots, and the French could be such shits. He didn't mind the snooty French intellectuals who felt they had a monopoly on the finer aspects of thought and style. But the others, the critics mainly, held their idea of what was black.

Much like Solange said. It was the same way in the States. You couldn't escape the bull. You could see it in how they looked at the black guys, the writers, and artists, who slept with their women. Somehow, sex took on a different flavor when the colored boy did it.

Some cats slept with ofay chicks as a way of settling old scores, getting back through them for the way the Man had treated them back home. Cole had sampled them, but it wasn't a taste that stuck. Some cats had two, three, even four of them stashed away, but his taste was queered by the memory of his brother, lynched for making love to a cracker chick who wanted to leave her husband for him. The ofay chick got knocked up by his brother, panicked, and went to her husband and insisted "the nigger raped her". A few of the local cracker men had waited for his brother to come home, had dragged him from his Buick, beat the hell out of him, worked on him with a knife, and hung him from a magnolia tree. The message was clear—nigger boys stay away from the pink at all costs.

Paris looked the other way with colored boys and foreign women, but if a Frenchie chick said a colored boy mistreated her, he was gone, kicked out of the country. No amount of pink was worth that. Cole didn't want to go back to the States. He couldn't. He'd die there or end up behind bars.

Weary, Cole finds a seat at one of the little bistro tables outside near the Coca-Cola sign. The thin dude who bar tends there sometimes chats him up on current events in broken English while he stands at the red-copper bar inside and remembers the night when they hung out at Haynes, a joint owned by an ex-GI who had also lingered in the City of Lights after World War II. All the jazz cats came through his joint. He went to Haynes for the soul food, especially the jambalaya, but a trip to Café Tournon meant chats on spook culture, hometown memories, and fiery arguments about art and music. That was cool.

"Your usual, Monsieur Cole?" the bartender asks flatly. He quickly serves the trumpeter two doubles of bourbon.

Cole downs them one after another while watching a clean-shaven black man in a brown suit sitting at another cafe table that is covered with a newspaper, two books, and a notebook. The man stares at the people walking on the street, the passing traffic, and general Parisian madness. Occasionally, a pen moves in his hand on the paper.

"Who's that?" Cole asks, sipping coffee. From this angle, he cannot see the man's face.

"Richard Wright, the man who wrote *Native Son*," the Frenchman replies, admiration in his voice. "There is no one with him today. I think he wants to be alone."

When Cole walks out, he gives the writer a quick glance, stepping close to his table so he can see what he is writing. But he cannot. Mr. Wright locks eyes with him. Cole nods, smiles, and says, "My brother."

The writer waves him over. Their exchange is very brief. They shake hands, Mr. Wright's hand is almost limp. Cole reminds him they'd met at the Monaco and again at Haynes's joint. He says he dug *Native Son* and *The Outsider*.

Everybody colored knows everybody else in Paris, For the most part. He tells Mr. Wright that he was surrounded by people both times, so they'd barely spoken to one another.

The books on the writer's table are Camus's novel *The Stranger*, a biography of De Gaulle during the war years, and a journal, *Presence Africaine*. He can't read Wright's writing on the paper—a scrawl of letters covering every line of the page. A photo of Wright, Sartre, and Simone de Beauvoir at the Shakespeare and Company Bookstore lays nearby.

"Where are you from in the States, my friend?" Mr. Wright asks as he drinks from a water glass, smiles, and rearranges the clutter on the table.

"From New York City. Musician."

"What kind of music do you play?"

"Jazz. Trumpet, like Dizzy. I'm playing at Le Cave over in Montmartre until next week," Cole says. He leaves after Mr. Wright promises to come to the club. He moves slowly, joining the citizens walking to the Metro. The subway. The Underground or the Tubes is what they call it in London.

That night, Cole gets a nice round of applause when he walks through the club to the bandstand. He holds his horn in front of him in tribute to the cheers. The dimly lit club is only slightly bigger than a jail cell, every inch of the floor covered with tables. Cole plays brass in the usual kind of quintet with a tenor and trumpet fronting the customary rhythm section, performing a bunch of old standards for the tourist trade and the locals.

Albert, the tenor man and bandleader, clears his throat, stares out at the crowd, and calls out the number, "I Cried for You". One of Lady Day's favorites. Cole thinks he wouldn't be there if he didn't need the francs. It is Albert's tune to toy with. The tenor man thinks he is the next Prez or Bean. Albert blows long, curling lines of sound with his horn turned to the side. Like Lester used to do it. Jean-Paul, the bassist, supports him with a few solid runs, full walking tones. While the pair plays, the other lays out, listening, and Cole rolls his eyes at Skeeter, a refugee from Detroit who plays the drums. Max Roach is the boy's idol. Then Cole steps to the mike with his trumpet blazing and responds to their lame jamming with chorus after chorus

7

of hot gutbucket-blues licks.

Skeeter pats his foot and smiles, his hands a blur of motion with the drumsticks. "Do it, baby, do it."

The trumpeter winks. The crowd cheers after each surge of notes. Cole blows harder and harder. The customers are on their feet, hollering and shouting encouragement. Albert looks pissed off, grimacing, holding his tenor and looking like he wishes it would all end. Showboating, Cole doesn't give a damn. His solo gets wilder and wilder, hitting unbelievably high notes and sustaining them. As if Skeeter reads his mind, the drummer crashes the cymbals and does a series of wild rolls on the snare to build the drama.

Waiters stop to listen. There is not a word of chat in the joint, and the cash register becomes mute as a strange quiet sweeps through the crowd.

Albert lifts his instrument to his lips and hops into the action. His expression says no way this boy is going to run him off the stage. He's never copped out of a cutting contest. For four choruses, they chase each other around Billie's tune, one note after another, sometimes quoting from pop tunes, grunts, and growls and slurs artfully placed to raise the hair on the back of the neck. The crowd is into it, clapping and whistling.

"Bring it home now," Albert hisses, blowing some low, dark tones from his horn in contrast to Cole's chatty, frisky trumpet runs. He signals to wrap up the number, which they do.

Albert, the bandleader, raises his hand and calls for quiet. "Thank you. *Merci, merci.*" He stomps off the start of the next song, *Night and Day.*

Cole runs away with this one too, blowing full-out on the trumpet, forcing Albert to follow up with some tricks of his own. He pauses for an instant between flurries, then starts blazing again, a vein pulsing recklessly in his neck. The two horns battle it out head-to-head until they roar through the final choruses to the end.

The crowd shouts its approval. This is what they like—spontaneous invention. Improvising on the edge.

After the show, Albert complains that he is losing control of his band, but Cole doesn't pay him any mind. He watches Solange. Solange, who will later drive her little Saab over to his hotel for some fun and frolic.

"If you don't like what we play, find another gig, Cole," Albert growls.

Skeeter laughs and says the best bands play outside the melody sometimes, stretching out.

"What was that shit you played tonight?" Jacques, the club owner, asks.

Albert frowns and tries to explain while the others laugh.

Cole puts on his dark glasses, pats his glistening conk and lights a musky-smelling Gauloise. Then he splits, lusting for his Congo cutie—Jacques's wife, Solange. His Negress, Miss Congo. A white man's wife. Her purple-black skin, jutting breasts, thin waist, and bubble butt. Long, shapely, dark legs under her thin cotton dresses. That thatch of black curly hair on her pubic mound. Her thumb-sized clit. The knowledge that her man knows about them doesn't bother Cole too much. Jacques once had them followed back to his place. Her man slapped her around when she got home. She ran back to Cole, all battered. She wouldn't let him hold her, and she did not cry. Oddly, she was proud of the damage her French man had done to her. It proved that the white man loved her, she said.

Another night, three of Jacques's imported toughs from *Pigalle* roughed Cole up as a warning to leave the African

9

seductress alone. That didn't stop anything. They were together that same night, when she told him about the day the Belgians from Leopoldville, the capital, came into the village and burned down all the huts and raped the young girls. Her too. A gang of foul-smelling Europeans in her body. But Jacques had saved her, got her a false passport, and brought her to the City of Lights. Married her and displayed her as his exotic nigger trophy from the Congo.

"Do you know what the Belgians call us back home?" she'd asked Cole, who shook his head. "I'll tell you. They call us *macac*, it means monkey. Everywhere you go, someone treats you like a *macac*."

Another day, it was cold, uncommonly cold for a summer day in Paris. Cole saw his breath rise like small vapor clouds. He thought of a couple he'd seen kissing and strolling hand-in-hand near the *Tuileries*.

Tonight, he watches a wasp crawl across the windowpane. His trumpet sits on the bed amid two ashtrays full of cigarette butts, sheets of manuscript paper for charts, an overturned bottle of Pernod, and an open suitcase. It's an old Buescher horn his grandpa gave him for his birthday with loose valves and leaks. But he loves its full, rich sound.

A knock at the door. It's Solange. In no time, she is naked in all her ebony magnificence, the color of dark-bruised plums against the startling white of the sheets. She tells him he is full of shit, for leaving, running away. He laughs. She says she imagines the head of his dick near her sex, so he teases her with it. She says she imagines him inside her, moving in an easy circular style, and the muscles of her vault tighten around him.

"Why do you want me, Cole?" she asks after, pinching her nipples. "Do you want me because I belong to someone else?"

He lights another cigarette and continues packing. He is a thin, dark man with a flat broken nose who loves his women purple or dark blue. Once, he'd sampled a blanc woman, Aurore, a blond singer from Marseilles, who rubbed his skin like a woman scrubbing a stain from her dress. At other times, she'd sniffed his underarms, his so-called man scent. She forbade him to use deodorant and inhaled the scent from his crotch. Sometimes, she'd told him she loved him. Sometimes, when he was inside her, he shut his eyes real tight and imagined the actress Simone Signoret or the singer Juliette Greco bucking underneath him—panting, submissive, with curvy white buttocks hot and wet. That trick never worked.

When Cole crosses the room to Solange, he takes a cigarette from her pack and places it between her lips. He feels her watching him, smoking. She does this until she finally seems bored and pushes him toward the bed. He resists. She breaks him down by stroking his dick through his pants, making it grow into diamond hardness. She has been drinking, heavily. Her breath reeks of stale gin.

"Jacques says he'll kill me if I see you anymore," she moans. "I think he means it. He'll kill you too."

Cole says nothing, only flips her onto her stomach, touches the moisture between her cheeks with his finger, and slowly slides into her. He drives into her like her husband would if he could. He pounds into her for every night he will miss her when he leaves. He rides her like it's the last time, which it is.

She screams, screams, and screams, but he is relentless inside her, twisting and snapping his hips into her until they come together, crying out as if stabbed in the heart, until she comes again, lifting her entire gleaming body to him, her purple hands desperately clutching the sheets.

In the time it takes her to smoke four cigarettes, Cole understands that he cannot leave Paris, leave her softness and the trouble that follows her like a bad scent. When she goes to the window, wrapped in his robe, he takes her in his arms and begs her forgiveness. But he must do what he must do.

Solemnly, Cole watches Solange put on some lipstick. The rouge coats her ample lips. The powder on her cheeks is white dust. The bed is soaked with their fluids, scents, and their sweat. At the lightest sound on the stairs, he presses his ear to the door, heart pounding, and listens for the men who will come to harm him.

He can't run anymore.

His Congo cutie finishes the repair job on her face, sits on his bed, and watches her lover with tears in her eyes.

Beautiful and Terrifying

It was the time of Japanese occupation, the early fifties, and the feeling of resentment was growing like weeds among the locals who hated the coming of democracy and the loss of feudalism. There was a reverence for the old ways and traditions which any foreigner could sense whenever Emperor Hirohito was mentioned.

Sergeant Davis arrived in Tokyo, a slightly-decorated black American soldier, a grunt with personal orders from the big man himself, General Durston. Or at least, the orders came from a second louie attached to the unit. There were killings of Japanese girls going on in the clubs near the American bases, nasty slice jobs, mutilations, and word had it that some colored troops were doing the butchering. Because of that, the nigger soldiers, as General Ike had occasionally called them when he was off-duty, saw their leaves canceled, off-duty privileges yanked, and all fun vaporized with a blanket restriction to base.

"I heard the Nips grabbed two colored boys in Osaka and damn near cut them a new asshole when word about the slaughter of these yella gals got out," the Lieutenant said to him, pulling him aside at the airport. "The big boys want you to wrap this one real fast. Things could really heat up."

"I know, sir," he said. "They don't want full-scale riots."

"Where did they bring you in from?" The white man, clad in a starched uniform, didn't look like some of the other soldiers committed to the reconstruction of the vanquished Land of the Rising Sun.

"Kyoto, sir."

"We spared Kyoto because it's some kind of holy place for these pricks," the Lieutenant volunteered, twisting his mouth cruelly. "I would have dropped the friggin' bomb on the bastards too. If I hear another person moaning about how we shouldn't have dropped a second bomb, I'll pull out my .45 and blow their brains all over the ground. Do you think the Nips would have just dropped one bomb on us if they had it? They would have dropped one on every big city in the States. You know I'm right."

He didn't answer the officer. Instead, his eyes surveyed the widespread damage caused by the regular night bombings in the final weeks of the war. Much of the place was still in shambles. Sure, some reclamation projects were going on, but for the most part, the devastation was still in evidence. Yank fly-boys hammered the hell out of it, as Operation Iceberg—the battle for Okinawa—drew to a close. Okinawa was within spitting distance of Nippon.

"I know some of the others told you I hate all colored because I'm white, but that is not the case," the Lieutenant said. "I have nothing against you or your race. Still, I don't think your people can handle the pressure of combat, listening to those bullets whistling overhead, the bombs falling all around. That's just how I feel, and a lot of other whites in this man's army feel the same way."

Again, the black soldier said nothing. His eyes might have flashed with serious disdain, but he buttoned his lips and remained mute. He was not going to let the white man ruffle his feathers, regardless of what he might say, regardless of what might be implied by the humiliating words—Nigger, why are you here?

"I don't get it," the white man said, shaking his close-cropped blond head. "How did you get old man Casey to be your rabbi? You have no combat experience that I know about. Tell me. I won't tell anyone. Are you guys bed-buddies?"

Behind them, a couple of B-29s were coming down for a landing, their engines roaring slightly before the final ascent. Pilots loved the fact that they could fly these babies without any flak or small-arms fire zeroing in on them. Their collective noise drowned out the continuing interrogation of Davis by the now red-cheeked officer, who acted as if he would knock the colored boy on his black ass if given a chance.

White officers, both Army and Air Force, walked by on the tarmac, grinning and nudging one another, looking happy that one of their own was reaming out a lazy, shiftless coon. At least that's how it seemed to Davis.

"Answer me, Davis," shouted the Lieutenant, the cords showing in his neck. "Remember I outrank you. How in the hell did you get Casey under your damn thumb? Answer me, boy!"

Davis knew this kind of race rage first-hand. He knew not to take the bait. He knew what Command would do if he slapped the taste out of this cracker's mouth, how old man Casey would feel if he gave in to the "lower part of his nature," and what this would mean to his military career in this segregated army. Negro leaders Adam Clayton Powell and A. Philip Randolph bitched and moaned about the beatings and murders of colored soldiers throughout the country—some lynched in uniform, others attacked at army bases—but among whites, it seemed only a handful were willing to put it on the line for their dark brothers. Political types like Henry Wallace and Wendell Wilkie; money man Marshall Field, and novelist Pearl S. Buck wanted to see a new world emerge. But this redneck was not one of those whites.

"I saved the General's life in Italy, and he found it in his heart to be generous," Davis answered, straightening his tie.

A jeep with two privates appeared at their rear, and one of the men jumped out, snapping off a salute. "Sgt. Davis, you're to report to HQ ASAP," he said, lowering his arm. "They are to present you with evidence and your new partner, sir. You are to come with us."

Davis got into the jeep, followed by the private. He sat ramrod still on the back seat, never looking back, never acknowledging the Lieutenant, who'd glared at him with burning eyes.

His thoughts turned to the murders. There was something sinister and evil about them. The last chief American investigator had been mysteriously struck by a bolt of lightning on a clear day as he'd left the grounds of a shattered temple just outside the city. He'd died at the scene. The bolt shot through him with such force that it seared away his clothes and knocked him several feet into the air. When onlookers glanced up at the sky, there was no dark cloud to be found, so the talk started that there was a curse connected to the case.

"The guy was a son-of-a-bitch anyway," one of the brass remarked, when Davis was going over the folder on the murders. "He probably pissed off the wrong person."

However, the Japanese said it was another sign that the Gods didn't want the Yanks in their sacred country, even the arrogant General Douglas MacArthur who was running the whole show and even bossed the Emperor around. He'd changed the rules concerning their treatment of their women, outlawed the local gangs, come down hard on the black market, and altered their traditional customs. He was rumored to have said about the murders, "Our boys have got to learn that fraternizing with the enemy, even with their women, has its consequences."

At headquarters, Davis met his new partner, Sgt. Gelb, who shook his hand and looked him square in the eyes before holding out a manila envelope marked "confidential". Gelb was tall, pale, with brown hair and exceptionally long arms and legs. His uniform fit him snugly, the creases looked like they'd cut to the touch. His black shoes cast off rays. It took Davis several minutes to follow what Gelb said. He had a thick accent, something regional, but he couldn't place where it was from.

"Sgt. Davis, we have a big problem here, mighty big," his white counterpart said. "The General put us together because he thought we would be able to get this thing solved in no time. He has great faith in you and your abilities."

"Can I see the folder, please?" He took the folder and walked over to the chair facing the door.

The information was startling, even shocking, for it said that four servicemen—one Negro and three whites—were missing, and four Japanese B-girls were dead. Tortured, branded, and strangled. What raised his eyebrows was that each woman had been sliced open, her heart removed, and the lips of her vagina stitched crudely shut, but not before there had been a great deal of sexual trauma. All the girls, ages seventeen to twenty-two, were found positioned on beds, bodies in natural sleeping poses, legs straight, hands folded neatly across their chests. Oddly, there was very little blood at the crime scenes.

"Have you read this, Sgt. Gelb?" Davis asked, sweat coming

to his forehead.

"Yes. What do you make of it?"

"Don't know. It's strange as hell. Either some devil-worshippers or a lone madman. The brass wants this mess cleaned up before it starts an international incident. I don't like it. I think there's much more to this than what is on these pages, much more."

Davis scratched his head. Looking at the black-and-white photographs of each female victim, he was stunned by the brutality of the deeds. "Can I ask you something?"

"Yes, what?"

"What in the hell happened to the soldiers?" That was the part that bothered him most. The disappearing soldiers. What was that about?

Gelb sat on the corner of a desk as other men walked briskly back and forth, busy with their own tasks. Their movement underlined their efficiency, intent, and discipline. There were no goldbricks among these handpicked guys, not at all. When there was no one near them, he spoke on the most mysterious element of the case—the detail of the murders that had everyone most baffled. "Pretty decent bods on those lovelies." Gelb leered. "Even if they are yellow. I like them small like that. Compact, bite-size morsels."

"So, what happened to the soldiers?" Davis repeated.

A look of horror crossed Gelb's pale face, spots of blood appeared on Gelb's cheeks, and his hands trembled slightly. The officer's Adam's apple worked frantically as if his throat had seized up on him. A few seconds passed before the white man replied.

The officer knew something, Davis thought, something that ate away at his sense of calm. Gelb's eyes widened as if the corpses of the mangled Japanese women were right in the room with them, but he didn't speak. Whatever he knew, he wasn't saying.

"All I know is that something weird happens every time one of these yellow girls get killed," Gelb said, in a hoarse whisper. "There's never...never...anything left of the men. No bodies. No guns. No dog tags. Nothing. Nothing but their shoes."

"Their shoes?" Davis couldn't believe it.

"Yes, don't you think that's odd and sad?" Gelb said. "Just their damn shoes."

It was odd, that was for sure, but Davis wasted no time on feelings. "Look. I'm going to go on over there." He itched to start.

"I'll join you later," Gelb said. "I've got to talk to a man here. We'll turn the place inside out until we find out what's what. Stay put until I get there. Okay?"

Davis reached for his gun, removed the clip, and slid it back into place. "Don't worry. I'll be there when you get there. But don't take too long."

"The *Tojo* is down that street, you can't miss it," a soldier yelled at Davis as he walked across the road. "The shouts and singing should lead you right to it."

He found it with no trouble. God, his feet hurt.

The grapevine had said service was first-rate, the girls pleasing to the eye, and the sushi and sukiyaki the best on this side of town. Most of the grunts ate there, watching the nimble Japanese waitresses move effortlessly around tables, carrying food with a grace usually reserved for other trades. It reminded Davis of another place, Kyoto, the old capital with its bounty of temples, gardens, inns, and shops. As far as Japanese towns went, Kyoto was special to the men in the service because the women were plentiful and easy. He knew that most GIs only wanted to use the local women there for sex—especially the ones in the bars and the others who hung around the PX—as they counted the days before their tours ended, and they could return home to their chaste all-American girls. But to these Japanese women, sex was about G.I. money. Yankee dollars meant survival. They flooded the cities from the countryside where there was no work and life was hard.

Once inside, he stood at the rear of the place, absorbing its boisterous Yank atmosphere. Soldiers drank and hollered, harassing the timid Japanese waitresses. Some older officers drank beer and teased the girls as they walked past, their slim hips swinging beneath flowered kimonos. A few of the guys danced with each other to the music of Vaughn Monroe coming from an old Philco phonograph, his baritone groaning of love lost and regained.

"Sgt., who are you looking for?" a white soldier asked, moving closer to him.

"Not you," Davis replied, looking around.

"Want a table?" the grunt asked. "Keiko, a table for this dark-complexioned gentleman!"

One of the waitresses, a slender girl in a yellow kimono, smiled and led him to a corner table which was all right by him. She sat him away from the others, obviously not wanting any trouble to arise from a Negro mixing with the others.

Davis sat, and the waitress returned with a bowl of rice and turnips, bits of chicken, and a bottle of cold beer. He whispered that he wanted some chopsticks, a bottle of warm sake instead of beer, and a small cup.

Two white soldiers in a nearby booth laughed and poked their lips out, making them bigger. Not the first time he'd seen this racial slur. Davis ignored them and turned his attention back to the waitress. "What's your name?" Davis asked, making his tone as cordial as possible.

"Keiko, Mr. G.I.," she said. "Is there anything I can do for you?"

He pulled out a picture of the last Japanese murdered girl, killed in a hotel not far from the bar. It showed her face. Her eyes were closed, and the photo gave no sense of the horrible crime she'd endured. The victim looked serene. Spiritual. "Do you know this girl? They say she worked here."

Keiko shook her head.

"Look at the picture again," Davis insisted. "Look closer."

Keiko's mouth started to say no again, but something changed her mind. "Her name is Miyako. Very sorry. I no know her at first. Bad, bad picture."

"What else do you know about her?" He wanted to be a real cop when he got out. If they allowed Negroes to be cops.

"Miyako, she special girl, not like others," Keiko said, a faint smile on her lips. "What happen her? Is she okay, G.I.?"

"No, she's dead." He said it with the finality it deserved.

Keiko swayed, obviously stunned by the news. "I know her from before. Her parents killed when American bombs come. I go with her to bury them. She not like the rest of us. Special...special."

"Yes, you said that," he said. "What made her so special?"

"I only know what I hear," Keiko said. "She have powers. She could move things without touching them. Shut off radio without touch. Stop clocks too. She could read mind even if you say nothing. Special...special."

Davis didn't know what to make of that. "When did you see her last?"

"Days ago." She looked away, seemingly still grappling with the news of her friend's death, having a hard time focusing. "A real special girl. She could make you pick up a glass if she wanted to. Walk a certain way if she wanted. Somebody say they see her toss a broom down in anger, and it turned into a snake. Real special."

"Did she go out with men?" he asked.

"Sometimes. Always with Americans, soldiers."

At that moment, Gelb popped his head into the bar and whistled once.

Davis stood and thanked the girl for her answers. She stood there, that dumbfounded look on her face, as he walked past her and out into the street. He thought it was strange that this Miyako woman would go out with soldiers, especially after it was American bombs that killed her folks.

"The girl's name was Miyako, worked here at the *Tojo*. She's been missing for two weeks," the white officer said in a rush. "The inn where the murders occurred is near here. I got a tip that we should go there around twelve."

They got into the car Gelb had arrived in, pulled out a map, and headed for the inn. Gelb drove slowly, telling Davis to look for the address. The inn was in a very damaged part of the city, full of debris. It was one of a few buildings still standing. The soldiers got out, walking with caution because of the many robberies that had been reported in the area. They stood outside, across the street from the inn, hunched up against the chill of the wind, watching their timepieces.

Gelb told Davis, with a low rasp in his voice, about Mr. Matsui. The old former priest had warned him, telling him the legend of a Japanese siren—a strikingly beautiful young girl—who possessed the power to seduce men and seize control of their wills and souls before loving them to death and taking them into the dark world.

Davis laughed at the story. "Sounds like a post-war fable. A fairy tale meant to keep the natives in line." There was a human being responsible for the killings. Nothing more, nothing less.

Gelb shook his head. "Matsui said the legend goes back to the Meiji Restoration time in the late 19th Century after Japan was emerging from 250 years of complete isolation from the outside world. It seemed the first of such deaths began just after the foreigners started arriving. Hundreds of foreigners died mysteriously. Matsui said the siren was a demon clothed in flesh, able to assume the appearance of any Japanese woman, and skilled in the art of love. Sex with the demon meant death. The old man said that once the seduction has begun, nothing or nobody can stop it." Gelb seemed almost convinced of the validity of the story. "He said the men no longer wish to live in the present, so they willingly invited this demon into their lives. This evil thing stalks her prey, waits for the most intimate moment, seizes her victim, and absorbs him until there is nothing left, not even a husk of abused flesh. It's as if she swallowed her victims whole."

"Do you believe that crap?" Davis asked, feeling a bit uneasy despite his better sense.

"I don't know. I guess not." Gelb swallowed hard, his Adam's apple bouncing. "But all their smiling and bowing makes me nervous. I can't help but feel we're one big joke to them."

"Lieutenant, let's say the joke is that there's a demon who takes control of women and uses them for its purpose. Why G.I.s?"

The officer laughed. "Why not? First, we bomb the shit out of them with these atomic weapons, and then we turn their world upside down. Who knows, maybe the demon's a Red. Wouldn't that be something if Moscow and the Russkies were behind all of this? Matsui said she was the perfect instrument of death, the spiritual revenge by the ancestors against the foreigners, especially the American occupiers, for defiling the sacred soul of Japan."

Davis didn't like anything about the case. Or Gelb. "Don't joke. This is serious. We have a killer out there, and we're no closer to capturing him than we were when we got here. What do you hope to find at this damn inn? It's probably another dead-end."

"Ease up, Sergeant. Or the siren will get you." Gelb laughed.

"I'm ready for whatever happens," Davis boasted, touching the weapon holstered at his side. "Demon or not, this baby will stop it in its tracks." Unfortunately, he really didn't believe what he was saying. Gelb was right. There was something spooky about this whole thing.

At five to twelve, a jeep pulled up. A soldier and a Japanese woman stepped out, hugged once, and went inside.

Gelb and Davis watched the couple stop at the front desk, and then go up to their room. When they spoke to the innkeeper, he was reluctant to cooperate. A threat to shut the place down brought the needed answers.

They went up to the second floor where the room was, careful not to alarm the other women and their clients. As they were about to knock on the door, they noticed it was open, just a tiny bit. Just enough for them to see the occupants of the room. They stood and watched the soldier shed his clothes while the woman, in a bright-red kimono, poured him a cup of sake. They could not see her face, only her back.

"All of you G.I. are in big hurry," the Japanese woman said.

She eased her garment away from her body, revealing small round breasts and a slender waist. "Me speak beri good, American-san. Make rove all night. No rush. Take time. Go easy, Daddy."

"Sure, baby," the white soldier said, his ruddy Irish face obviously the result of drink. "We have a good, good time, yes?"

The woman seemed preoccupied, pouring him more sake. "Good time. Are you married, Joe? Got wife back home?"

"Name's not Joe. It's Allan," the soldier said, panting like he was fighting back a desire to toss her on the bed. "And yes, I have a wife back in the States."

"Very good. Good to have wife," the woman said. She laughed. "You real cute, G.I."

He lifted his butt, and she removed his pants and underwear, her hands going through the motions with practiced grace. Then, she took off her clothes. She was a real pro. Her long, tapered fingers seized his privates. She stroked him before taking him into her mouth. It didn't take her long to bring him close to climax. When he seemed completely distraught with longing for her, she sat on him, locking her legs around him as she moved almost manically against his pelvis.

He moaned and tried to match her movements, but she was too much for him. When he went one way, she went another. Their coupling seemed frantic. The G.I.'s mouth opened wide, a screech rising before her hands covered it. He bit her, gasping loudly for air, but her hands remained fast. His teeth drew blood that ran between her fingers, along the back of her hands, and onto her waist.

Davis was excited at first, watching the coupling, but he was also afraid, too terrified to run, his fear growing with the increasing volume of the dying soldier's agonizing screams, a continuous background noise that perfectly matched the gruesome sight of the man's flesh, bone, and blood being slowly pulled by an unseen force into the spinning vortex of light and evil emitting from the Japanese woman writhing atop him. Davis felt something like a strong electrical charge coming from the pair on the bed, powerful enough to stand the hair on his head on end. Gelb stood next to him, his mouth agape. Despite the legend talk, neither had been prepared for this startling reality.

"She's killing him, killing him," Davis said, moving to enter the room.

Gelb grabbed his arm.

"We've got to do something."

"We can't. Let's watch. See what happens," Gelb said.

Suddenly the soldier screamed at the top of his lungs, a tortured scream, ear-shattering as if he was being turned inside out. The room filled with a blinding light and a fog of some kind.

Gelb and Davis fell back, holding their hands before their burning eyes, down on their knees.

There was another scream, more terrifying than the first.

It was Davis who got to his feet first, drew his gun, and rushed into the room. "My God, Gelb...Gelb," Davis yelled. "You've got to see this!"

Gelb ran into the room. He grabbed the wall, legs shaking like uncooked spaghetti. He stared, then looked away, squeezing his eyes closed.

The Japanese woman lay on the body, her heart ripped open, and that feminine space between her slim legs stitched shut, just like the others.

Davis and Gelb stood close to the bed, but her lover was nowhere to be seen. Only the man's highly-polished black shoes remained, government issue.

"Look at her face!" Davis shouted, holding the photo of the dead girl up for his partner to see. "Look at her!"

Gelb snatched the photo from him. "Damn, it's that Keiko dame. Same girl! Oh shit, what's going on?"

Davis sat heavily on the floor next to the dead man's shoes, found a cigarette from the pack in his shirt pocket, and lit it. "The General won't believe this. This is some mumbo-jumbo shit. Nobody will believe this." He heard Gelb throwing up in the corner of the room, retching like there was no tomorrow.

The dead woman's face swiveled toward Davis, the features of Keiko slowly morphing into those of another Japanese woman, someone he had never seen before. She spoke to him without moving her lips; her voice echoed in his mind. "For you G.I.s, we Japanese women are all the same. All whores, only our faces are different. Even then, you cannot tell us apart. Remember this, soldier. Suffering reminds us we're alive, reminds us of what is right, and even death reminds us that there is a price for what we do to others. Remember what you have seen. And you shall be spared."

Davis swallowed hard, a ripple quivering his stomach like he was about to piss his pants. By the time, Gelb straightened up behind him, it was all over. The body of a Japanese woman they did not know lay on the bed, ripped, bleeding, and stitched. And all that remained of her lover was his shoes, neatly placed on the floor.

Gelb ran from the room, heaving.

While Davis listened to his partner scramble down the stairs, he lit another cigarette, his hands trembling, his head shaking.

27

This shit was unbelievable. How would he ever explain it? How many Yanks had this thing killed? Her words made a sick sense to him. His people had dropped A-bombs on Nagasaki and Hiroshima. She was repaying a cruel debt. Karma or some shit like that.

Another flash of light filled the room. He stared at the dead woman on the bed as she sat up. The hole in her chest closed, and the stitching between her legs vanished. He tried to get up and run but found he could not.

The woman, now whole, placed her feet on the floor, smiled slyly and asked, "What is your name, G.I.? You want good time. Good, good time? Me make love to you all night."

Davis struggled to get up from the chair, but his body seemed leaden, like a collection of dead flesh. He screamed and screamed and screamed.

Irresistible

Lightning crackled in long, twisted bolts of illumination across the endless stretches of fertile, flat land in the distance. This was Kansas, the fabled territory of Oz, Dorothy, and her little dog, Toto.

She kept her bloodshot eyes on the winding asphalt road ahead, trying to beat the rain the dark clouds promised would come. On both sides of the old Dodge, golden lakes of grain stretched as far as one could see. An occasional farmhouse or silo dotted the line on the horizon. The car coughed, rattled, and spat as she pushed it to the limits of its endurance, attempting to get to lodging before nightfall.

Nowadays, she spent much of her time spreading the gospel of the Lord, zigzagging across states, teaching the holy word wherever anyone would allow her to use their vacant field or building. Kansas was the fourth state on her current tour across the Midwest. It was a grueling business. Sometimes, a good neighbor—one of the newly converted lambs—would take mercy on her and invite her to take a spare room rather than travel on the road in the dark. Sometimes, she was not so lucky and would have to sleep in her car. Since she'd left Chicago three weeks ago, she'd worked most of the towns around Kansas City—everywhere from Lawrence, Overland

City, Topeka, and all the way to Emporia. Tonight, with luck, she'd stop in Iola, a small place in the middle of nowhere.

Before God, there had been her addiction to men. Always men, of all shapes and sizes. She had come to New York City more than ten years ago to audition at a modeling agency after a scout had seen her photo in one of the local papers in Detroit, a cheesy shot of her standing next to a new Ford. Her mother watched her like a hawk during that first stay in the big city, never letting her daughter out of her sight. The older woman lectured her endlessly about the perils of being seventeen in a metropolis like New York City without anybody to protect or guide her. Oh, the temptations and sins that awaited her. Everybody told her how beautiful she was, a combination of Cindy Crawford, Iman, and Veronica Webb. Something exotic, something original. She had no idea how obsessed with beauty the entire society was until she listened to her handlers and her mother discuss how much her face and body would bring in financial gain doing runway and print work in Europe.

Often, she wondered what her engineer father would have thought if he'd lived to see her on the way to fame and fortune. On her tenth birthday, he'd been killed instantly when a car driven by a teenager, hopped up on three forties of chilled malt liquor, lost control of his vehicle. It jumped the curb and ran him down. The loss left a void in her that would never be filled.

Yes, she was tall, pretty, clever, and healthy, but was she worth the thousands of dollars they paid her hourly to walk up and down in front of gawking people? Her mother continually cautioned her that looks didn't last. "Take advantage of them while you can. Nothing lasts forever. That's our only guarantee in life." Her mother always concluded her beauty speech with this little pearl of wisdom.

Beauty carries such a heavy price. Nobody would have imagined she spent so many weekends alone in a darkened room in front of a television. Nobody would have imagined she'd been dumped more than once by men intimidated by her looks or dreams. Nobody would have imagined how often guys wooed her with lofty promises of fidelity only to flee at the first note of commitment or real intimacy. It was all so fleeting—the magazine covers, the chic nightlife, the fancy vacations, the high life. At nineteen, she was a has-been, burned out, with a serious cocaine habit and memories of an Italian boyfriend, Mario, who'd overdosed on heroin. The good times were behind her. When things got bad, her mother deserted her, just like she'd always known she would. Life in the fast lane was too fast.

Before Mario died, one night had damaged her trust in men forever. She'd come home from a photo shoot to a living room where her boyfriend sat with another girl, Laura, a model he'd been working with for a session with *Elle*. The yellow girl was totally nude, her skin flawless except for the pale imprints where her bikini had been. Her man was dressed in his boxer-briefs. They smoked joints on the bed, twisting around each other, giggling. When she entered the room, they didn't stop what they were doing. After five puffs of the potent ganja soothed her shock and gave her a powerful buzz, she let them undress her. Soon, Laura's head was between her legs, her narrow yellow behind up in the air. After a time, they changed places. For her, it was like a dream, fuzzy and disjointed as if she watched herself in a strange porno movie. From that day forward, it was all downhill, ending with Mario stretched out on the bathroom floor, dead and bone-white, his crystal-blue eyes rolled up in his head, a spike in his arm.

Ten years later, all her big dreams of becoming a hotshot actress with a big-time movie career had evaporated because the drugs had left their mark on her looks. The little cutie-pie girl from Detroit, who had once been transformed into a supermodel by a brigade of agents, stylists, and photographers, was long gone. In her place was an older, wiser, and sober woman determined to find redemption in this world before going on to the next one.

Turning her life around had not been easy. It took the near-death experience of an overdose at an after party in the back room at Cosmos, a trendy Soho nightclub, to bring her to the Lord. That autumn night, she'd been snorting coke for more than six hours straight when her nose started to bleed, and her heart began racing as if she had just finished the New York Marathon. Disoriented, she tried to get to the ladies' room, thinking she'd splash water on her beautiful face, when everything went black, and the floor came up to smack her in the mouth. A short time later, she was loaded in the back of an ambulance and rushed to St. Vincent's Hospital where doctors twice shocked her back to life after her heart shut down.

While she was fighting for her life, she saw herself stretched out on the gurney, doctors and nurses battling to bring her back. Nothing they did seemed to work.

Her father, dressed in his usual splendor, looking flush for a dead man, gave her a red rose from his suit lapel. "Elizabeth, you can live, or you can die," he said. There was a sly smile on his long, narrow face that she would never forget. "Your choice."

Dead or alive? That night, she chose life. That night, she found the Lord. And she'd been working for him every day since.

On the highway headed for the next town, she plowed ahead as the sky grew darker, letting memories of the past play quickly and quietly across the screen of her mind. She reached for a can of soda on the front seat, taking her eyes off the road for only a second. A slender figure popped up in front of her car just as she glanced back up. The car's brakes screamed loudly, and she lurched to a stop scant inches away from the man, who leaped back from harm's way.

He stuck his head in the window of her car. "Lady, can you give me a lift to the gas station? My car's up ahead about two miles, out of gas. It looks like it's about to rain, and you're the first car I've seen in about an hour."

She looked him over carefully. A woman alone had to be cautious about picking up a hitchhiker or a supposedly stranded motorist on the road. Still, covered with dust, he appeared not to be the type that would cause any problems. Tall and slim, the man was dressed in a dark suit, shirt, and tie, but wore sneakers. That worried her. His head was bald, and his body appeared to be quite solid under the cloak of the suit. It was his face that captivated her, unwrinkled and without any sign of the ravages of time. He wore the face of a child, innocent, and pleasant to look at. She calculated his age to be somewhere in his early twenties.

"Where are you trying to go?" She hadn't paid any mind to the signs along the road.

"Redding. It's up ahead. So small it's not even on the map." He stuck his hand into his jacket and left it there when she scowled.

"Are you from there, this Redding?" she asked, keeping him in her line of sight.

"Yes. I'm driving back from Kansas City from a job interview," he said, almost cheerily. "A salesman's job. I don't know if I got it. The guy said he'd call me in four days."

"I was just in Kansas City a few days ago," she said, watching an airplane dust a field far off in the distance, swooping down out of the clouds to release its load of insecticide.

"That's why the bees are disappearing, the insecticides," the man said. "Bug sprays. It's killing them. That and mites, mobile phones, even the loss of their hives."

"What?"

"Did you know bees in this country pollinate more than fourteen billion dollars' worth of seeds and crops yearly?"

"What crops?"

"Mainly vegetables, fruit, and nuts."

"How do you know so much about bees?" She still didn't trust him.

"I raise them on my place," he replied. "I have a few hives."

She motioned for him to get in, which he did after swatting some of the dust from his clothes. "I didn't know bees were so important."

"Yes, they are," he said. He smiled. "Bees keep the reproduction of plants going. Keep them surviving. If the bees vanished off the earth, some say man would only have four years left. With no more bees, there would be no more man."

"Or woman, for that matter," she said.

"What do you do?" the man asked, reaching absently into his pocket again. "Do you live in Kansas City?"

She laughed and swerved to avoid something on the road, then straightened out the wheel. "I'm an evangelist. I travel around the country, teaching the word of God."

"That must be tough on your family, with you on the road all the time," he said. "What does your husband say about you driving all around preaching?"

"I'm not married. I'm too busy for that kind of thing."

"I thought all women wanted a husband, a family, and a home. It seems like the normal thing to do. Surely God wouldn't mind if you took yourself a man. It doesn't seem right for a person to go through this world alone. Without love."

"Well, my personal life takes second place to the work of God." She thought about what he had said. "Sometimes, it's not what you want, but what he wants. God wants me to serve him, taking his word to sinners wherever I find them."

He laughed and said he'd been rude. "My name is Ray. Ray Draper, originally of Abilene and now of Redding. What's yours, lady?"

"Reverend Elizabeth Little," she replied. "Pleased to meet you."

"Reverend Liz, answer me this," Ray began, speaking slower as if choosing his words with great care. "Do you miss men? Do you ever miss being loved and adored by a man?"

Sure, she missed it. Not that she'd ever tell him what it was like, sleeping in a different bed every night, with your body throbbing and aching from the lack of touch. It had been so long since she'd been with a man. Maybe six years. Maybe she'd forgotten what to do if the opportunity arose. And then there was the matter of her calling, her ministry, the divine business that left no room for indulging the flesh. If she strayed from the path and took herself a lover, how could she say she was a true disciple of the Lord? He'd saved her once, and she owed him. Maybe this young man was a test of her faith, of her resolve. She couldn't let herself be swayed by temptation.

"I've lived a full life and tasted every fruit," she said. "But that was before I found the Lord. That's all behind me now."

"It's sad." He said it as if he pitied her. "Your God won't let you be a woman. I know people who worship or preach the Bible, and they live a good, normal life without denying themselves anything. I don't think they're evil people."

"Everyone has their way of serving the master." She pulled into the gas station that seemed to appear out of nowhere. "This is my way of serving. I don't question him."

"How do you know this is what he wants you to do?" he asked.

The man at the gas pump took a fistful of cash from another man in a truck.

"You might have it all wrong. It sounds to me like you're punishing yourself for something."

She wanted to answer the man, but he jumped out of the car and walked over to the gas station attendant, who appeared to know him. As she watched him, they started quarreling. The attendant took a swing at her passenger who quickly knocked the guy down with a punch to the face. He went through the man's pockets and took the money from his hand.

She revved up the engine to pull away, but Ray ran in front of her car, waving his hands. There was a gun in one of them. He pointed it at her, and she lifted her foot off the gas pedal. He walked around to her side of the car and pushed her to the passenger side.

"Why did you do that?" She fought down her hysteria. "Why did you hit him?"

"He owed me some money. Also, my wife and kids ran off with him. He's lucky I didn't kill him. That's what I came up here to do, kill him. He got off easy, I think."

"Where are you taking me?" she asked, as he pulled back onto the road.

He didn't answer her. The car sped over the road for almost two miles before he turned into an alley behind an old abandoned roadhouse. They barely made it inside before it started to rain, a downpour. She watched his hand with the gun and wondered whether she could make a run for it. Her mouth tasted like copper, full of fear. She remembered seeing no deserted car on their way to the gas station.

He found an almost-full bottle of Scotch in one of the cupboards and two glasses. He offered her one. She shook her head, but he still held out the glass. His request that she join him in a drink was not a question; it was an order. Her body shook while she stared at him pouring her drink. She'd feared a moment like this for much of her time on the road. Many nights, she'd pass a tavern or a roadhouse during her travels, and it took every bit of inner strength to keep going on. Now she had no choice.

"You must have some past to be so scared of everything." He motioned for her to drink up. "What are you so afraid of?"

"Myself. You wouldn't understand that. I've seen your kind of man before."

"What kind of man is that?" He gulped the last of the spirits.

"The kind of man who no longer believes in anything, not even in himself," she said. "The kind of man who wants to corrupt and poison everything he touches. Am I right?"

"Maybe." He covered his face with his hands. He said nothing else and continued to drink until he looked sleepy.

She drank one last drink with him and went to the bathroom where she stripped down, showered, and washed her hair. At first, she wondered what he might do to her, but then she dismissed her fear and surrendered to the gentle spray of water. God was with her. No harm could come to her, not with Him by her side. When she returned, he said she could have the bed, and the sofa would be his for the night. He promised her there would be no funny stuff. It didn't take long for her to fall asleep.

He got up and walked to the bedroom door and stood there, listening to her soft breathing, watching her lying on her side.

He could see Elizabeth was truly a splendid woman for a beauty nearing thirty-five, with a pleasing face, great legs, and a magnificent, mature set of breasts. The temptation to satisfy his curiosity was so intense that when he turned to leave, he did not.

Instead, he knelt by her bed and moved his hand lightly along the length of her exposed leg. He continued his explorations of her warm flesh until she sighed in her slumber and flipped on her other side, turning her rear to him. Carefully, he slid under the sheets next to her, still in his underwear. As soon as his skin touched hers, he got hard.

Her eyelids fluttered. She was now awake, pressing every inch of her body into his. There was no doubt she wanted him, the first man she'd laid in bed with for longer than she'd said she could remember.

The solitary glow of a burning candle lit the room. He was not a man who approached lovemaking as a chore to be finished as quickly as possible. His fingers hoisted the back of her blouse, gently unsnapped her bra, then massaged the softness of her shoulders and back.

He placed patient kisses along her spine, on the rise and ebb of her hips, and the satin mounds of her rear. His intrusive fingers, his kissing, and cuddling, intended to fuel the pitched battle between her desire and virtue. He smiled to himself because her body responded although he suspected she fought every impulse to make his task of seduction any easier. She barely opened her eyes to look at him as he hunched over her with his solid spear of skin in his hand. Once inside her, he moved his hips up and down slowly, building her passion skillfully like a campfire. When he almost slipped out, she twisted under him and held him fast within her. She met each penetrating thrust. The blood roared within his veins, his sex puffed up to a size where it hurt him to be in her, but he couldn't help himself with the background music of her moaning and talking filthy to him. He felt his seed rise, yet he could not come. She bucked and rolled on the bed after he withdrew from her without warning.

With a graceful motion, he lifted her from the bed and carried her kicking to the bathroom where he placed her against the sink, facing away from him. Now he climbed on her, gripping her around the waist as if frightened of being thrown, and danced into her with gyrating hips. There was a touch of something urgent and hysterical in their second coupling. Soon, he shouted and sagged into the wall behind him, his sex sputtering.

At last, she felt like a real woman, no longer a prisoner of her past. This unsuspecting man had resurrected the emotions pent up by layers of deception, disillusionment, and disappointment. Afterward, relishing the wonderful feeling of intimacy between them, they stayed in their individual poses, in the tiny cell of the bathroom.

He smiled. "Was that all right?"

She laughed and wiped the sweat from her forehead. How

could she answer him? Sure, she was grateful for what he had given her, but there was no future between them. His face wore an odd, hurt expression. She flinched when he took her hand gallantly, kissed it, and begged her to stay with him. No answer existed for his question, so she gave him none. In her heart, she felt a tenderness for this stranger who had revived her sensuality, but she fought down an urge to surrender to him and submit to his every wish and command. She answered his probing eyes and questions by putting her arms around his neck, kissing his serious face, and crying as she never had for any other man.

They talked for hours in the darkness, side by side on the bed. Sleep finally came to them both. The sound of a car pulling up outside awoke them. Soon, someone knocked on the door. Ray slid on a shirt, hopped into his jeans, and walked barefoot toward the living room. She sat up on the bed and grabbed her clothing to cover her nakedness. Two beefy white policemen stood in the doorway, quizzing Ray about his whereabouts the previous day, ultimately informing him that he was under arrest. Ray protested but to no avail. The officers handcuffed him, and his muscular chest gleamed with sweat.

One of the officers found her purse on the sofa and fished around inside it. "You don't care who you screw. Do you, Miss Little?"

She burst into laughter. With the eyes of all the men fixed on her, she faced them, feeling wild and a bit unhinged. She opened her blouse and adjusted her bra over her full breasts. Still laughing, she pulled her dress over her legs.

The men fidgeted nervously, seeming uneasy, now faced with the tantalizing spectacle.

"Boys," she said, her voice low and sultry. "Take your

prisoner and go. Bye Ray. Thank you for a really wonderful evening."

"What did I tell you, Reverend Liz?" Ray said, as the men marched down the path to the police car. "I screw up everything, tarnish everybody and everything around me. That's what I do best. Screw up. I'm sorry for all this." Just the roughneck sound of his manly voice caressed something in her.

She remained in the doorway until the car was just a dot on the highway. *"You don't care who you screw, Miss Little?"* That nonsense remark by the officer only made her want to laugh again, only made her want to return to the tousled bed and think once more about the fireworks of the previous night. Ray had really sparked something inside her. She would never deny herself again, not in this life. The woman in her was alive, awake. Armed with this glorious knowledge, Elizabeth Little started laughing, laughing until her entire body shook from the force of it. Certainly, the Lord wouldn't deny her this small moment of bliss.

The Other Cheek

They searched for the fiend that night. They searched for him that morning, but the manhunt yielded no fruit until they discovered him shaking and trembling with fear and pain a few hours later in the fire pit of a cold furnace.

They handled him roughly, like a colored man who had done wrong, tossed him about, and slammed him hard against the wagon which would take him to his last confinement.

The three whippoorwills sang the saddest blues ever. Or that is what some people remember about that tragic night at the once-majestic structure of architect Frank Lloyd Wright's prized Taliesin. Blood flowed among the mound of ashes in the living room. The master builder Frank Lloyd Wright did not think about the well-being of Gertrude and Julian Carleton, the staff members he hired upon the referral of John Vogelsang, the owner of Midway Gardens, an entertainment complex in Chicago. In the spring of 1914, the man designed the buildings after a pattern based on the famed German beer gardens. The Germans would flock to the center in great numbers later. Chicago was full of them, the Heinies, as they called them.

Everybody talked about the massacre. The rich white folks who were slain in Mr. Wright's pleasure dome, at the hands of the dark foreigner who was in this country at his whim. They gathered around the dark man, Carleton, slouching against the wall. He clutched his throat with one hand. His clothes were in tatters. Dirt and blood splattered across his chest. The pressure of what he had done weighed heavily on him.

"What is your name?" asked one of the white men.

"Is your name Julian Carleton?" yelled another.

The black man said nothing.

"Were you serving dinner to the guests of Mr. Wright when you did this heinous thing?" The stout white man shoved his prisoner against the wall, making him wince from the pain. "When did you set fire to the Wright bungalow?"

He remained mute, staring dully toward the wood floor.

"Do you know who you killed? The most respectable and honorable white people in this area? Did you know that, nigger? You murdered them in cold blood. You killed Mrs. Mamah Borthwick and her two young children, John and Martha Cheney. The young people were only eleven and nine. Did you know that?"

The other man slapped Carleton's face, whipping his head around almost to his spine. "How could you kill the kids?" he shouted. "How could you? You black bastard."

The Negro slumped, the sweat dripping onto his legs. But he never spoke.

"You killed three other adults and another child, only thirteen-years-old." The one who'd slapped him punched him in the stomach. "Do you hate white people? Is that why you did it?"

The stout one grinned evilly. "You wanted to kill Frank Lloyd Wright. Didn't you?"

Carleton shook his head as if he was in a trance.

"Did you know Mr. Fritz of Chicago had to leap out of the

43

window to escape your rampage, breaking his arm, his body covered with burns?" Another hard slap.

Carleton kept shaking his head.

The stout one turned Carleton's perspiring face toward his crimson one, placing his fat fingers under his chin. More white men entered the room. One held a newspaper with the banner headline: NEGRO MURDERER OF SEVEN, showing it to all his peers who looked like they could kill the criminal without a second thought.

"This is what happened," the stout man said, his face near the Negro. "The men were being served dinner in the small dining room while Mrs. Borthwick and her children sat on the porch. You asked Mr. Weston, the foreman of the bungalow, for some gas to clean a rug. Weston gave you permission. But you poured the gas on the walls and along the door and lit a bright fire, so they couldn't get out. You wanted to trap them. You wanted to burn them up. Right?"

Carleton fiddled with a raw burn on one of his hands.

The stout one continued, poking one of his fingers into Carleton's cheek. "The white people tried to escape, flee to safety. You grabbed a hatchet and started to maim and kill them, slashing and cutting them as they ran toward the door and window. Mr. Fritz dived through the window before you could get him. Two other people followed him out through the glass."

Two other men held Carleton fast and punched him repeatedly. He put up no resistance. He still made no sound.

"You killed them, one by one, with the hatchet," the stout one shouted. "Butchered them. You ignored their screams, their pleas, their cries. You nigger son-of-a-bitch!"

Carleton slouched and let the tears come.

"Do you know what you did?" the stout one yelled. "Do you know what you did?"

The Negro covered his face with his left arm, sobbing quietly.

"You killed Mrs. Borthwick with a single blow to the skull," the stout one said. "Then you killed the children. Her family couldn't recognize her badly charred body. But you didn't get them all. Two of the survivors ran to the next house for help. Most of the wounded died immediately. Others died later at the hospital."

"Why did you do it?" the one who'd hit and kicked him the most asked.

Inside the shell of the Negro man, thoughts raged in his agonized brain. *You know why I did it. De whites always fornicatin in de house. Mr. Wright stole that pasty-face white lady right away from her family, from her man, from everythin'. He knows he is wrong. He knows de lady is evil. De Bible say it was wrong. Everybody had to die. They can beat me until de cows come home, but it can't bring dem back. Nuthin can. I knows evil. I knows evil nevah sleeps.*

"Why did you kill the children?" another man asked. "Do you hate white people, is that it?"

Carleton closed his eyes as if to blot out everything in the room.

"Why would you do this to Mr. Wright after he's been so good to you?" the stout one said. "He took you in, gave you a job, and treated you like a white man. Niggers never had it so good. Talk about biting the hand that feeds them."

The Negro looked at the white men and knew he would not live to see the day out. Maybe they would lynch him. Maybe they would shoot him. Maybe they would do both. But he had cheated death. They could not do anything to him now.

The world knew Mr. Wright as a devoutly religious man with an ego, arrogance, and a sense of style. When the judge asked him to identify himself, he called himself the world's greatest architect. On the train from Chicago with reporters, he soon discovered there was something more tragic than the fire at his beloved Taliesin. Multiple killings had taken place in the buildings he had constructed as a monument to his dear Mamah. He leaned on his son, never turning to look at Mamah's husband, Edwin Chaney, who had come along to claim the bodies of his children.

Mr. Wright only cried when he was alone. When he walked through the ruined bungalow, he smelled the acrid odor of the gas and the lingering scent of dark smoke. A rumor had it that Mamah had not paid Carleton. Another said the Negro had a disagreement with one of the staff. His workmen had built a row of plain wooden coffins for the dead. He did not see Chaney off at the train station with the boxes containing his young children.

With Taliesin in ashes, Mr. Wright attempted to put together his thoughts about the killings, the love scandal, and his shrinking reputation. He wondered if he could ever design any buildings again. He wondered if he could face his friends and associates.

He started jotting on the back of an envelope. The article covering the catastrophe in Sunday's *Chicago Tribune* told the story of a brilliant deception, of the murderous black striking out young and old in the heat of madness and malice. He thought about the bright, shining faces of Mamah's children and imagined the horrible moment of their death. *We have lived frankly and sincerely as we believed, and we have tried to help others to live their lives according to their ideals.*

46

No one should expect to have a potent influence in our children's lives for good—and they had not. The paper said the children had lacked the atmosphere of an ideal love between father and mother—nothing that could further their development. But how many children had more in conventional homes, he wondered? Mamah's children had been with her when she died. They had been with her every summer. She felt that she did more for her children in holding high above them the womanhood of their mother than by sacrificing it to them. And in her life, the tragedy was that it became necessary to choose the one or the other.

Tragedy never derailed Mr. Wright. It always provided lessons and parables for him. He frequently used it as emotional fuel or an impetus for ambition and ego.

Meanwhile, Julian Carleton, the Wright hired hand, had cheated death at the hands of his white captors. When he was caught on the furnace floor, he had swallowed a great quantity of acid. He stared with horrified eyes at his bloody fingers and at the congealed blood across his shirt. The treatment at the jail was anticipated. The burning of his mouth and throat pained him to the core of his being, for the acid had rendered him unable to eat and talk. The white folk got nothing from him. He never said a word.

Mr. Carleton died a month later, carrying the secrets of the killings to the grave.

The Astral Visitor Delta Blues

Alligator, Mississippi, July 11, 1961

Frank Boles wasn't thinking about aliens, spaceships, or anything else extraterrestrial on that hot moonlit Delta night he went to Minnie's jook joint. He shrugged his broad John Henry shoulders and went upstairs, past the frowning, bent man who checked him in at the door. Not tonight. No, he wouldn't think about the chits he owed at Mister Wiley's store, or whether his daughter Bue got herself knocked up by that Dixon boy or if Mister Tyree was going to throw him off his place for hitting the peckerwood down at the feed shed over in Oriole. Not tonight.

Tonight, he was going to raise hell and worry about heaven tomorrow. The rocking sound of music could be heard through the beaverboard wall, good down-home blues. A few people standing at the entrance stepped aside to let the tall, gaunt sharecropper pass.

After a brief survey of the dance floor, Frank decided he didn't know anyone there, not even the sad-faced man sitting by the window, dispensing paper cups of corn whiskey. No, he didn't know anyone, but he could be wrong in the dim light.

Inside, a bright-skinned man bobbed his head as he pounded a piano into joyous submission, accompanied by another blue-black man playing harmonica and a tricky-fingered guitarist, who looked sleepy. Stationed in front of the musicians were two singers, a couple, slickly dressed. Frank chuckled as he maneuvered his way through the tightly packed tables, noting how the lights caught the glimmer of the male singer's head. Both entertainers seemed drunk or close to it, and Frank was in the mood to follow suit.

He chose a rickety seat in a corner, not too close to the stage, but far enough so that he could get a good view of the room. He ordered a whiskey and surveyed the club. Everybody was talking, singing, and dancing all at once. Among the revelers, Frank spotted a few of the Holiness people, the backsliders, several drifters, two or three medicine men from the Dixie road show parked just outside of town, and a couple of odd-looking strangers in snow-white suits. They were on the other side of the room, but nobody paid them no mind. Frank searched the mob for a glimpse of his old friend, Isaac, but the joker was nowhere to be found.

Frank settled back and let the whiskey and the music wash over him. Every tune sounded faster than the one before it, and the crowd wasted no time catching up. One woman in a low-cut dress was snapping her long fingers over her pretty head. Frank grinned as she shook her wide hips to the steady beat. Many of the old heads there did a dated shuffle, nothing to work up a sweat, though. Once and a while, someone would step out from the group, do some spins and twists to leave the others wanting more.

Frank wasn't much of a dancer himself, but he loved to watch. Lovers were snuggled up, belly to belly, whispering in each other's ears. He sat safely to the side, grinning. Often, in the middle of a tune, some bad bucks would cuss loudly, pushing and shoving, or going for pistols. Frank wanted no part of that, so he preferred to watch. Most players that worked at Minnie's knew its rowdy reputation and usually set up on a stage near a window, ensuring their escape if the crowd got out of hand. Word was out about the gun play and knife-throwing that sometimes took place.

Veterans said it was a tradition carried from slavery times, the wild and raunchy weekend rumble. Onliest thing Frank did exciting on a Friday night before he came to Clarksdale was throwing a brick at a guy who cheated him at cards.

Glass in hand, the male singer swept back a couple strands of processed hair from his glassy eyes and sauntered across the stage, wiggling his hips to the ladies' delight. The band switched to a slow, simmering blues. The singer paused as if feeling out his audience. A shout from the back of the room sent heads spinning. Frank's lanky back stiffened, but the scrawny singer went on with his introduction to the next song, a suggestive ditty by Tampa Red. By the volume of noise from the cheers, Frank could tell it was a house favorite.

More stragglers came in, humming along. The singer rocked back on his heels and sang the bass part of the song, while the woman did the falsetto.

"I've got a gal, she's low and squatty,
I mean boys, she'll suit anybody,
And everybody likes her, 'cause she loves so good."

Paper cups made the rounds in the crowd as the couple cut up something awful, bumping and grinding against each other. Frank surmised that the mean-looking crooner was riding her when they weren't doing the shows, probably a nice roll too.

People on the floor seemed to love their insinuating antics and singing, clapping and stomping in tune with the sizzling words of the song.

The woman broke into moaning, twisting, and wringing her hands, stroking the man all over, then stroking herself. The crowd whooped in excitement.

Frank sat up straight when the woman gapped her legs while telling the crowd just how she loves so good.

After she ended her solo, her partner came back to wrap it up, beckoning to her suggestively, his conk hair flying behind him.

The audience sang along, chuckling at the raw lyrics as if it were their first time hearing them. Frank drank glass after glass of spirits, enjoying the ruckus. On through the night, the singers and musicians worked the crowd to a fever pitch, with no letup. Frank got into the energy of the music and the place, doing his old buck-and-wing dance, rocking back and forth on one leg while the folks egged him on. He leaped high and came down into a dancer's split with both legs straight out under him like the stretched arms of a clock. The folks loved the jig and gave him a round of clapping. He took an uneven bow, swaying dangerously. Lawd, he loved a good time.

"Big man, you put on quite a show out there," said a gal Frank knew from a jook near Drew. "You sure got big hands. Look like you could break a tree in half with them."

"That ain't all that's big," he flirted, after his vision cleared enough for him to see her seductive smile, watching her soft brown eyes and cinnamon face, her soft curves barely concealed under a tight yellow skirt.

"You plumb crazy, fool." She laughed. "I'm here with some hick from over in Jackson, but mebbe we can get together." She nodded toward the door.

Frank was tempted for a hot moment, but as the room wavered around him, he knew he was in no condition to fight his way out of the club. He turned her down and watched her wiggle away from him into the crowd before he tossed down one last gulp of his brew. He had reached his limit of drink about an hour ago, but he stayed on to the last, tossing down cup after cup of the clear, burning liquid. Shortly before three in the morning, he tried to make it home, staggering in the street under the power of the alcohol. His head was throbbing. Finally, he wobbled into the hallway of the colored hotel where he had a room. He pulled himself painfully up the stairs, one step at a time until he got to his floor.

Once inside, Frank stumbled to a rickety chair and sat on it, with his aching head in his large, calloused hands. Everything on his body pained him as if he had just finished a long day in the fields with his old white cracker boss standing up over him. That peckerwood had a way of getting his goat more than anybody else in the world. Frank was slumped in the chair, just staring into space when it happened.

The light came from behind him at first, outlining a shape, forming a silhouette. What attracted his stare was the silvery glow around the figure, the pulsating center of it. Blinding light. A voice called from somewhere out there, and a paralysis crept over Frank, rooting him to his chair. The voice faded back into the blackness where it had come from, the light broke apart and bounced back and forth, then the luminous face of a man dressed in a white suit, a bright white suit like those strangers at the jook, appeared from within the glow.

Something about the man transfixed Frank, but he couldn't say what. The voice returned, deeper, richer. Words, but a language he didn't know. He didn't understand them, tractor

52

talk, machine blabber, white noise. He covered his ears, but the words penetrated his flesh, ruthless, all-powerful. This enchantment, this spell, this hant.

Frank watched the frightening vision from the chair, trembling, shaken to his very core. He was drunk but not so drunk that he now saw things with his eyes open. The buzzing continued in his ears, filling his head and moving down into his chest. Was this a devil, one of those hants his grandmama used to talk about when he was a boy? Whatever it was, Frank felt it knew him, knew all about him—his thoughts, his secrets, and his sins.

The voice came again, louder and louder. Frank noticed that the face never changed, the lips never moved. The emptiness around the man peeled back with a deafening roar. The trance embraced Frank and wrapped him in its arms. All sensations invaded him as the voice echoed with a sound much like the scratchy music of birds' wings beating fast. Then there was a smell, a smell he recognized, the scent that came after a heavy rain. Frank felt his heart stop, then it continued. The man in white sat motionless, like stone, shutting his eyes until there was only the fluttering of the lids. Jacob and the angel, Moses and the burning bush, the two divine beings of vengeance at Sodom and Gomorrah.

Frank watched the man produce two green seeds in the palms of his hands, his fingers outstretched and flat. The man smiled knowingly. The seeds took root into Frank's dark flesh and huge leafy flowers—light orange with gold trim—pushed up toward the ceiling. He heard the song of their sprouting and knew then that he only understood life to a point. He was insignificant. Soon the flowers vanished, and a blue-white beam of light replaced them. The man smiled again, and his eyebrows lifted, his white suit glowing. Frank watched him for a moment while the beams of different colors now flowed into a triangle, each hue separated, collecting in a cube shape, dividing in half, and finally swirling in a circle.

Frank sensed the hair on the back of his neck rise as he pitched forward and fell to the floor. He shivered again and again, unable to resurrect himself. There was nothing but fear within him. For a minute, his mind filled with sinful, bleak thoughts. He imagined his own death. He would have rather driven a dull knife through his pitiful heart or sent it in a crimson crease across his throat. Suddenly his body went stiff and bitter tears came to his eyes. Staggering, he hoisted himself, shuddering in a coughing fit, then wiped the foam from his lips.

His body was covered with strange marks, odd burns, and markings as if he had been branded. His fingers hovered over the marks, afraid to touch them. At the window, he saw something outside, floating, like vapors, whirling lights in the open field near the parking lot. Lights that glowed like those in his room then vanished.

All that next day, Frank thought about what he had seen. When he went to the colored diner for breakfast, folks were talking about flying saucers, people from outer space, men from Mars, and odd happenings all through the Delta the night before. People said they saw spaceships land, cattle gutted, pigs turned inside out, two men hauled up into the air and vanished, large stretches of field scorched by something, and a known Klansman found naked and babbling like a fool behind his cabin in Sunflower County.

"Frank, do you believe any of this outer space mess?" Cephus asked the sharecropper in earnest. "Any fool can see there ain't nuthin in the Good Book about no damn flying saucers. Where is any of that junk in the Book of Revelations or the Song of Solomon? No way."

Frank heard the guffaws of the four black men sitting along the counter, dressed in their field clothes. "Hey, somebody says the Russians sent a monkey up there and brought it back. Say the ape got more sense than most people."

Frank didn't say a thing. He picked at his breakfast, his fork unsteady in his rough, trembling hand.

"Satellites, Sputnik, robots, spacemen...hah!" Cephus roared, his bass voice booming throughout the tiny diner. "Let me tell me tell you something. My old Aunt Cat says this space stuff ain't nothing but some Hollywood jive, 'cause we all know they can do anything out there. Change a man into a wolf or a bat, make things disappear, bring back ancient times...anything. Saw some foolishness on Mr. Tim's TV the other night where the great big lizard tore up the whole world, and here I woke up, and the world is still here."

The quartet burst into knee-slapping chuckles. "Ain't nothing but white-folk magic." Isaac smirked. "And weak magic at that. We see right through it like we did those Greek fellas come through here with that carnival last year when they were supposed to make that narrow-ass olive women be gone, and she got caught in some trapdoor. She screamed so loud they had to send me out yonder to get her out. Just phony all the way around."

Frank nervously watched the men chuckle, knowing most colored folk laughed because they'd been to the picture show and knew the white man could make anything seem real. Hollywood magic.

Isaac slapped him on his back, saying that he only believed what he saw with his naked eyes and nothing more. He laughed weakly, forcing down a forkful of grits, his hands wavering. Not long ago he would have agreed with Isaac, but now everything seemed suspect. How could he explain that something had visited him overnight and taken two toes from each of his feet and left no wound! And the bizarre markings on his chest and thighs? Something was up there in his blasted room with him, and it wasn't something he conjured out of corn whiskey. It was something unnatural, something unearthly.

Well, something was not right in this place. And probably around the world. What was the answer to that riddle?

Closing Arguments

In a corner office not far from the White House, a group of well-dressed men sits around a bank of tape recorders, telephones, and typewriters. A hum, a buzz, and a distant ringing in the machines alert them to calls. The Bureau has assigned them to wiretap every phone communication taking place in the Oval Office. The surveillance is to satisfy the whim of the Director, Mr. Hoover. He doesn't like Martin Luther King.

Saturday, August 15, 1964 (4:15 p.m.)

President Lyndon B. Johnson: Did someone get King on the phone?

Staffer: Yes. The connection will be made in short order.

Johnson: (clears his throat): Martin, I want you to call off all the marching, demonstrations, and protests. The country is wondering what's going on. The good ole boys don't like it. They're resisting all your efforts. Believe me, the Congress is controlled by them. Are you there, Martin?

Martin Luther King: I am here.

Johnson: Did you hear what I just said?

King: I heard, Mr. President.

Johnson: Martin, I know I can persuade, charm, and talk a bird right out of a tree. And I'll be honest with you, Martin, I've been a master of the Senate, but I don't rightfully know if I can get these rednecks to vote like I want them to vote.

King: I hear you have them in the palm of your hand.

Johnson: That's an overstatement. But you don't know you're up against. These die-hard white folks will bring the country crashing down before they give full citizenship to the Negroes. They don't want to see the colored eat at the same restaurants, go to the same churches, go to the same schools, drink from the same water fountains and live in the same neighborhood as white folks. They want you people to stay in your damned place.

King: Where is our damned place, Mr. President?

Johnson: Just hold off, Martin. Just hold off until I get the good ole boys in the Congress to come around. It won't be easy, but it can be done.

King: My people have waited too long, much too long.

Johnson: I know that, Martin. I'm just talking about patience. Just let the power of democracy take its course.

King: Mr. President, too many people have been killed, murdered, lynched. Churches have been set afire or bombed. Children have been hurt badly or killed, men and women humiliated and degraded. My people, my people, Mr. President.

Johnson: What do you want me to do? Tell me that.

King: (Silence)

Johnson: All right, Martin, you keep going out there and keep doing what you're doing, but I can't guarantee your safety.

King: (sounding slightly angry) Dogs, fire hoses, clubs, angry words, and deeds. Burning crosses. The government must govern for all the people.

Johnson: I know, I know.

King: Mr. President, I know you have a mighty hill to climb.

Johnson: (Silence)

King: I'll always remember how you went before the Congress just five days after JFK was gunned down in Dallas. Those words will always stick with me: 'No memorial oration or eulogy could more eloquently honor President Kennedy's memory than the earliest possible passage of the civil rights bill for which he fought for so long.'"

Johnson: I recall that speech too. I remember the pale, red faces of my southern Dixiecrats when I stood there before them.

(reciting) 'We have talked long enough in this country about equal rights. We have talked for one hundred years or more. It is time now to write the next chapter and to write it in the books of law."

King: That's good rhetoric.

Johnson: I realize that, Martin.

King: Mr. President, if it hadn't been for you, we wouldn't have had a civil rights bill back in 1957. President Eisenhower didn't want to sign it. Wouldn't have if not for that Little Rock crisis.

Johnson: Goddammit. Excuse my French, reverend.

King: That's all right, Mr. President.

Johnson: Boy, I miss those days. The horse trading, the gabbing in the cloakroom, the flattering and the pleading. Yessir, I miss it. That was real politics. Being President is not what it is cracked up to be. Everybody wants to be top dog. That's for true.

King: I wouldn't know about that, Mr. President.

Johnson: That damn bastard, Bull Connor, with his fire hoses and clubs. Using them on those colored schoolkids. Nobody likes to see kids being whupped and hurt. No matter how hard your heart. Birmingham, oh Lord.

King: Some people do.

Johnson: A. Philip Randolph. What outfit is he with? He's been around a long time.

King: He was affiliated with the Brotherhood of Sleeping Car Porters. He's a good man. He's done a lot of good.

Johnson: He is a proud old fella. I used to see old colored men like that in Texas and throughout the South. As a proud as a bantam rooster.

King: What are you going to do, Mr. President?

Johnson: Martin, I've got to unstop the toilet. The civil rights bill is tied up in the House Rules Committee. We've got some firm Democrats on our side, but the majority of the opposition are Southerners. Hardcore Dixiecrats. I tried to use the argument with the Republicans that they are supposed to be the party of Lincoln, but they don't want to hear none of that. They don't want to give the bill a hearing. Or an up or down vote.

King: I suppose they'll use a filibuster against it.

Johnson: I know. The opposition did a filibuster to stop the passage of the bill in 1957 and 1960. Who knows? Maybe they will just make a lot of noise and give up. I got a good man on the case. We worked it out with Mike Mansfield, of Montana, to get Hubert Humphrey to steer the civil rights bill through the south.

King: I've always felt Humphrey was a good friend of the Negro.

He always says the right things.

Johnson: I usually don't trust liberals, but I don't think Humphrey will let the bill go off the tracks.

King: (Silence)

Johnson: I worry about those bomb throwers (LBJ's term for liberals). They will gum up the works if we let them.

King: I trust them because they have their hearts in the right place.

Johnson: I must live with this. I know, when I deliver the civil rights bill, Southerners will never forget how I rammed this law down their throat. The crackers will leave the Democratic Party and join the GOP. What we do today will have repercussions for generations to come.

King: That's a big price, but America needs this bill. Democracy should not have any contradictions. Do you think so, Mr. President?

Johnson: They say you're a pretty bright boy, Martin. Everybody loves to hear you speak.

King: (switching the subject) What about George Wallace? He's a big problem. He's stirring up more hate.

Johnson: I have Hoover working on something to neutralize him. We have bigger fish to fry.

King: You know that's right, Mr. President.

Johnson: In the papers, the NAACP's Roy Wilkins said I am still offering liniment to cure a tumor. He says I wanted a watered-down bill that had no teeth in it. Do you share his views, Martin?

King: No, I don't. I think you want the strongest bill possible, Mr. President.

Johnson: Thank you for that, Martin.

King: But I know you'll not be able to cleanse people's heart with a stroke of a pen. There'll be some hard work to be done.

Johnson: My weapon is the telephone. Your weapons are marching and sermonizing and protesting.

King: The struggle continues.

Johnson: They say you've been in jail over sixteen times and stabbed once near the heart. That even your home has been bombed three times. You want more protection, Martin? There are some crazy folks out there.

King: No, thank you. Probably my wife and family would have said yes, but I think I have enough security. Thanks just the same, Mr. President.

Johnson: Martin, you're a man of great faith. I respect you for that.

King: We believe that God will make a way when there seems no way. We have faith that things will work out.

Johnson: But sometimes we must give God a little help.

King: All this hate is a tragic case of human injustice. Jim Crow is a collection of immoral man-made laws, sir. Jim Crow was not created by God. These white Southerners know in their hearts that segregation is morally wrong. It's a sin. They want to turn back the clock. I wonder if they will suffer a crisis of conscience. Do they have guilt?

Johnson: Sure, they do.

King: I never get tired of telling this story. Do you want to hear it, Mr. President?

Johnson: Yes, Martin. I got time.

King: There was a dark moment in Birmingham when Bull Connor and his deputies were clubbing the children. A white policeman pushed a little, colored girl, maybe seven or eight years old, who was walking beside her mother. The white policeman asked the girl in a rough voice, 'What do you want?'. Without hesitation, the little girl looked him in the face and answered, 'Fee-dom.'. I love that. A child shall lead them.

Johnson: (pausing for a moment) Do you have any Reds, commies, in your outfit? The FBI says you have plenty of them in your organization. They say you have some among the leaders of your outfit.

King: No sir, I don't. I know the John Birch Society and the White Citizens Council say I'm a communist agent. That's not true. I am an American, and I believe wholeheartedly in this country.

Johnson: Some of your people like the radicals, H. Rap Brown, and Stokely Carmichael, say I'm a bigot. They see me as a white southerner, a cracker, a peckerwood. You hear their speeches.

King: I don't hear them say that, Mr. President.

Johnson: Hoover got his boys all over these Klan killings in Alabama and Mississippi. You got to admit that.

King: You must be twisting his arm. Hoover doesn't like me. He thinks I'm a communist agent trying to overthrow the government.

Johnson: No, he doesn't. He just thinks you're a tomcat. Do you have a lot of ladies?

King: (Silence)

Johnson: I won't tell. Anything you say over these lines is confidential. What about that Bayard Rustin boy? Is Hoover telling the truth about Rustin having affairs with he-shes and faggots?

King: I don't know his business, Mr. President.

Johnson: (switching subjects) Martin, I'll try to get this bill passed, but it won't be easy. You don't know what I'm up against. Hell, Goldwater's unstable. Did you know he had two breakdowns?

King: Mr. President, you've been very successful.

Johnson: And this damn Vietnam mess. I don't want to get bogged down in this war and get a lot of boys killed. Secretary McNamara is trying to talk some sense into the Viet Cong. What do you feel about Vietnam? Do you think we should get out?

King: One thing at a time. I'm just trying to get the civil rights bill passed.

Johnson: Fair enough. I'll tell you this. The Joint Chiefs say we should bomb the hell out of them. Bomb military and industrial targets, mine the harbors, even form a naval blockade.

King: Uh-huh.

Johnson: Martin, I'll twist their arms and tell them that they cannot let your country down. This kind of thing looks bad for America. I promise you that I won't compromise the bill. Thanks so much for chatting with me, Martin. I knew we saw eye-to-eye on many things. Say hello to your family for me, especially your lovely wife, Coretta.

King: Thank you, Mr. President. God bless you.

Tell No One

I. Jean, the heretic

It was a late-night call. Something frightened her. Many said she was paranoid, afraid of shadows and boogeymen, but she knew something was out there. She had stirred up the Enemy, made them pay attention to her, made them target her.

Her friend had seen her only four times recently, but he talked to her almost every other night.

She said FBI men were following her everywhere she went, trailing her to stores, salons, even to the market.

Her friend spoke to her at the market over the cantaloupes and other melons, bunches of purple grapes, and small mountains of golden apples. Her voice, soft and precise, told him there was so much to tell—secrets, conspiracies, plots, and grand schemes.

A man drifted up near them, his hands in the pocket of a gray suit, turning toward them as if using his body as a hearing aid.

Jean Seberg, the internationally known star of *Bonjour Tristesse* and *Breathless*, fingered a loose strand of her short-cropped blonde hair out of her pale face. She smiled mysteriously and walked in the other direction. The nondescript man watched him, her friend, rather than the popular actress.

A dark car pulled up near the curb. The man walked over to the car and which contained two men. They pointed at Seberg, who had vanished around a corner of the crowded Paris street. "Pick up her trail."

As Seberg's friend was about to leave the market, the mysterious man moved toward him. "Can I talk to you for a minute?" He pulled out an official card stating he was police. "You were talking to Miss Seberg just now. What you were talking about?"

"What?" He was angry now. This harassment must stop. He saw what Jean meant.

"Can I ask you what you were talking about?" He repeated his question rather snidely. His English was very good. He sounded American.

"I don't think that is any of your business."

People walked around them, going on their way to jobs, theatres, restaurants, whatever. He wanted to slug the man, but the policeman had friends in the car. They would be back. What did the French call them? *Flics*. He hated cops.

"We could take you down," the man said, patting a gun under his coat. "You should cooperate if you know what's good for you. Are your papers in order?"

He shook his head at the man in disbelief, turned on the sidewalk, and walked away.

The man let him go.

"They have my phone bugged." Jean had warned him. "I'll call you from the street or from a friend's place. We must talk."

At the time, he'd thought she was joking. Now, he knew better. He had met the Enemy, and they were not playing, but what was their objective?

Jean said they wanted to crush her, to humiliate her, to

neutralize her. Her words made his hair stand out on his head.

Seberg had called him a little after midnight. She had been slightly out of breath, her words rushed and choppy, her tone sad. Car horns and the bustle of people told him she was not alone.

"They want me dead. Dead," Seberg said. "They want me to do something stupid. Well, I'm not. Let me tell you. I couldn't before."

"Tell me, Jean," he replied. "You know I won't tell anyone. You know that."

"You have to promise to tell no one," Jean pleaded. "The FBI planted that story about me having a baby with this Hakim guy, who was in the Black Panthers. I had gone around with him, but we weren't really lovers. I just loved to hear him. He made a lot of sense. I know how Hoover and those FBI bastards have it in for me. I gave a little money to the cause, but so did Jane Fonda and Vanessa Redgrave. And they're making it hell for them too."

"Where did the story appear?" he asked.

"Salim, you were a Black Panther a long time ago," she asked, not answering his question as if her mind couldn't cope with too much at once. "You got out when Huey Newton went to jail. The government wants to see you and all your kind behind bars. Do you remember Hakim?"

"I remember Hakim, but I don't know him well," he replied. "I know some Panthers wanted to kill him because they thought he ratted them out. Told a lot of party secrets to the feds, I don't know."

To Jean, Hakim was a thin black man with comfortable features, a beard and goatee, and big hands and feet. She liked to tease him about his dancer's ass. "He was an organizer in the

BPP's Chicago office and one of Fred Hampton's inner circle. His work on the west coast didn't bring him into the presence of Raymond Hewitt, the Minister of Education of the Party, but he was involved with Eldridge, Bobby, and David Hilliard. You know I love my men. Hakim fascinated me for so many reasons." Jean laughed, a little girl's giggle. "Did you know I had an affair with Sammy Davis Jr., the singer?"

He was surprised. "No."

"Have you ever been in jail?" she asked, sounding very innocent.

"Yes, when I was a kid, once for stealing a car, a Buick Roadmaster," he said. "And three times, all on a weapons charge when I was in the Party. That's it."

"What did the feds want you for?" She was always curious.

"I don't want to talk about it," he said. He didn't like anybody getting in his business. Including Jean.

"I get it," she said. "When I lost the baby, Hakim reappeared in Paris after Romain and I split up. I was staying in a separate wing of his house for a while. This whole business of the baby had taken its toll on us. I ended up in a nursing home. When I saw him, Hakim told me he had been living in Morocco with this Englishwoman, Gail Benson, but he was now broke and had decided to come to Paris to help me through the ordeal."

"Why do you think he came back?"

"He needed money, and he knew I was a soft touch," she replied. "So, he showed up at my apartment in Paris. Romain told him I was in Spain, but he found out I was in a nursing home. Hakim told me my husband and the doctors were conning me about my mental state, saying I was unbalanced."

"Were you nuts?" he asked. "You had just come through the baby ordeal."

"Maybe I was," she said. "Who knows?"

"So, what did Hakim do?"

She laughed. "Hakim packed me up and took me home with him and Gail. I was still obsessing about the baby. I really wanted that baby. Hakim saw some photos that a photographer had taken of the funeral and snatched them from me. He threatened to destroy them. I tried to take them away, saying they were the only thing I had of my baby, and if he loved me, really loved me, he'd let me have them. He said I was acting. He said I didn't even love the baby. I had them bury the baby in a glass coffin so everybody could see the child was white and not black."

"Are you kidding me?" He was stunned by her admission.

"Hoover planted the story that I was having a baby by a black man and not by my husband," she said, her voice conveying her still-fresh anger. "It was only the way I could show the world that I was not lying. Even my husband didn't believe me until I showed him the baby. They ruined my life. They ruined my career. They ruined my marriage."

"Damn them," he muttered. "And it was the FBI, you say?"

"The stress they put me through was so strong that I mis-carried," she said, weeping. "It was a little girl. I named her Nina Hart Gary. I named her after someone in the family who had signed the Declaration of Independence. I was very sick with this baby. I even had transfusions, but the hospital knew it was a troubled pregnancy because of the stress. The FBI and a nasty *Newsweek* article did that to me."

"Oh damn." He couldn't believe what he heard.

"Hakim asked me to marry him then, and I told him no," she said. "When I didn't do what he wanted, he turned against me and left. And then he arrived after everything was over, turning up at the nursing home, taking me home with him, and forcing me to tear up the photos of my baby's funeral. I was an emotional mess. He knew it too."

"Jean, how are you feeling now?"

"I'm still screwed up," she said. "Hakim manipulated me. He said he had to fuck me as a part of the cure. Only black dick could cure my white grief. So, Hakim, Gail and I went to bed, and this strong, bearded black man tried to cure us—these two white cunts, as he called us—with his black dick. I hated it. I think Gail did too. I was fed up with Hakim's shit. Miraculously, Romain arrived on the scene."

"What did he do?"

He heard Jean lighting a cigarette. The clink of glass told him she was drinking too.

"Romain got together with Hakim and said he was being sought by the flics and that he could get him out of the country," she said. "My husband did it to save me. He knew Hakim had me under his control. I was totally out of control. I was nuts, and he knew it. So, Romain got Hakim and Gail out of the country and put me back into the nursing home. I was in a sorry state."

"I had heard Hakim was a guy out for himself," he said. "He was a snitch for the pigs. An informer for the FBI, they said. I don't know if that's true, but he was a greedy bastard who wanted to be rich and was motivated by his hate for whites. And that Party wasn't about that. We wanted to get the whites involved so we could defeat the pigs. The media didn't tell the truth."

"You know, I joined the NAACP back in my hometown in Iowa when that was not done," she said, her voice brightening. "This was America's Corn Belt. I knew it wasn't right the way whites were treating blacks. I hated it."

"Saint Joan, huh?" he joked.

"No, Saint Jean." She laughed. "I'm tired. I want to get some reading in before I go to bed. It relaxes me."

"What are you reading?"

"Duras's script for *Hiroshima Mon Amour*," she answered. "Call you tomorrow."

II. Limbo

Jean Seberg arrived at his apartment in Montmartre, a dingy two-room walk-up, above a garish burlesque show. It was drizzling. Girls stood around outside with their umbrellas, in the doorways, and in the streets, trying to lure the customers to the many hotels where they could go for an hour. The actress, wearing big sunglasses, had on a big raincoat, a white frilly peasant blouse, and jeans. She carried a bag with a bottle of wine, bread, cheese, and a copy of *Paris Match*. Her hands shook the bright red umbrella over his faded wooden floor.

He was happy to see she was smiling, but then he remembered she was an actress. A fine one.

"I've got to pee." She laughed "Point me to the bathroom, or I'll squat and use a pot. I've got to go so bad."

"In there," he said, taking the bag from her.

She closed the door behind her as he poured a drink from the bottle. He stood at the window watching the women pacing the street, the umbrellas obscuring their faces and upper bodies, their hands occasionally motioning to the men. The cabinet door was open, so he took down another glass.

"You all right in there?" he called to her.

No answer. He walked over to the door and listened.

"Are you okay in there?" he called, louder this time.

No answer. He opened the door, frightened that something had happened to her, but found she had stripped down to her bra and panties. She had the whitest skin he had ever seen, pure porcelain, its whiteness almost transparent under the harsh electric light.

She looked startled at his appearance but relaxed. She trusted him, he knew. "I had a chill from those wet clothes," she said. "That umbrella is all show. It's no damn good. I was soaked. You don't mind that I got out of my wet clothes?"

"That's all right." He stared at the beautiful woman with her pleasing face, boyish breasts, and great legs. When she bent to put her shoes side by side, he noticed her backside, round and firm, like a runner.

He left the doorway and went to the table for the wine, taking another glass and filling it. She walked over to the bed, wearing his robe, the dark blue terrycloth one. The covers on the bed were piled up in a jumble.

"You need a cleaning woman," the actress joked.

"I have one."

"When is she coming in?"

"On Thursday." He laughed. "I'll prepare the provisions and serve you. I see your friends followed you. I saw them from the window."

"Fuck them," she said. "They don't give me a minute's rest."

He spread out three sheets of an old newspaper on the bed and brought the glasses and the bottle. She placed them on a table after pulling it over to the bed. The wedge of brie cheese and the knife were on a plate, and the knife, under her artful hands, sliced the bread. They laughed like two children on a picnic, the gray worries of the day outside this place of calm and refuge fading away.

She squatted on the bed like an old Indian squaw and spread cheese on bread, handing it to him. "I didn't finish the Hakim story. He thought he was a sorcerer. He hated whites, and I think he hated blacks too. I know he hated himself."

"I think he thought he was a bad nigger," he said. "He was a chump."

Her finger wiggled in front of him. "I hate that word."

He took a swig of wine and bit into the bread with the cheese. "The Party thought you were one of the white stars who really made a difference. Masai even said you were cool. Your heart was in the right place. Brando was cool too. The FBI must have watched all you cats to see which ones were loaning your houses in Beverly Hills out for fundraisers for the Party."

"Yeah, I know," she replied. "I went to a party given at Leonard Bernstein's home in New York for the Party once. He was cool too."

"I was there," he said. "Maybe that was where we met. I would have noticed something as fine as you." He smiled as she blushed.

Their eyes met while they drank silently. He thought both of them thought the same things.

"Vanessa told me not to get involved with the Panthers," she said. "She warned me, said if that leaked out, I would not get any more jobs in Hollywood. She thought the anti-war movement was all right, but she was very cautious about anything involving civil rights. After all, she was a foreigner."

"Hoover found out," he said.

"Wiretaps. Damn fairy," she cursed. "I gave the Panthers a lot of money. I thought they were trying to do good. Free schools, free healthcare, free books, everything. I liked what they stood for. Do you know the code name they had for me?"

"No," he said, watching her drink the wine.

She took small bites of the bread. "Aretha." She chuckled. "I love her singing. Oh man, her singing gives me chills."

"I'm a Billie Holiday man myself," he said, watching her watching him. Something could happen if they were not careful. That man-woman spark was flickering between them.

She wiped his mustache with a tissue. "You got wine on it. There."

He smiled, hoping to keep the conversation from Hakim and the lost baby, hoping to steer it clear from anything that saddened her, hoping it would be a pleasant time. "Did you know Elaine? Elaine Brown?" she asked.

"Oh yeah, a stone fox. Very pretty. Hung out with Huey. And Ericka Huggins. I had a real jones for them both. If I could have got them alone, I would have went for broke, for sure."

"I got to know Elaine real well." She took another gulp. "Very sweet."

He thought back to Chicago, that winter of 1969, the FBI plot, and the death of Fred Hampton, the chairman of the local Party. They had always ridden in a convoy of cars, one car out front and another bringing up the rear. They were always armed. They had enemies. On that December night, Fred and Eldridge had been feuding over some white folks tossed out of the Chicago office. Fred thought the white radical were counterproductive to the cause of black liberation. It was an early morning raid where Fred was repeatedly shot in his sleep.

"What are you thinking about?" she asked.

"The Sixties. We almost got them." He would have been there at that house if Fred had not sent him to be with his wife, who was expecting. Fred's wife, Deborah, was expecting too.

She had laid there next to his bloody body after his murder by the feds.

The funeral of Hampton was an event, friends, dignitaries, politicians, and even members of the P-Stone Rangers, formerly the Blackstone Rangers. Civil rights leaders Jesse Jackson and Ralph Abernathy spoke at the burial, and thousands of people surrounded the casket. He cried in the basement of a fellow Panther, sobbing and shaking with the anger and grief before the funeral. He couldn't let them see him cry.

"Well, I didn't finish my Hakim story." She gulped down wine and poured another glass. "Want to hear it?"

"Not really." He didn't want any crying jags.

She stared at a poster of a Coltrane taken in a club, probably the Village Vanguard in New York. His body bent in a bow, holding the horn aloft. Her eyes penetrated the black-and-white photo before she said anything else about Hakim. "I loved Coltrane when he was playing the horn with Miles's band."

"Very cool."

"You know, Hakim's girlfriend was Gail Benson, the daughter of a British MP," she said, looking at him now. "He renamed her Hale Kimga. The woman would have done anything he wanted her to do. She was his slave."

"Dick-whipped, they call it," he said.

"When Romain got them out of the country, they knocked around Europe and then went to the West Indies, where they met Michael X or Michael Abdul Malik," she said. "He was very strange. Hakim left her, going on long trips, and I don't know how he ended up in Boston, but he died. In fact, he was brutally murdered by some Mau-Mau group."

"I heard about them." He put a slice of cheese into his mouth. "They were a black radical group, like the Panthers. They were all vets from Vietnam. Yeah, I know about them. But what happened to Gail?"

Well, Michael X went by the name of Michael de Freitas, and he rented a house near Port of Spain in Trinidad," she continued. "I guess Gail had been left alone by Hakim. Anyway, Michael went berserk and stabbed Gail and a local kid. They say Gail was stabbed and buried alive. The police found the graves in a garden near the house. Just horrible, huh?"

"Damn. Unbelievable." He drank the wine and burped.

They laughed. "When did all of this happen?" he asked.

"In 1972, they found them," she replied. "They executed Michael X in 1975. You know, they had to do it. After all, the woman was the daughter of a British MP. He had all these establishment connections. Powerful connections."

Her fingers moved lightly along his exposed arm, sending sparks through his dark flesh. She smiled, and there was no doubt she wanted him.

"Jean." His voice crackled.

She rolled over on her side, turning her ass to him. As soon as her skin touched his, he felt himself get hard. He gently unsnapped her bra, its hooks coming apart very easily, and stroked the pale softness of her shoulders and the nape of her neck. She moaned.

"Do you like me, Salim?" she asked. "Really like me? Tell me the truth."

"Yes, I do," he said, his voice husky.

He smiled as her body responded as if only his mouth against her skin mattered. He eased his fingers along her thigh, wondering what it would feel like to be inside her. He put his lips on the down of her throat, sensing its pulse point.

"Once, when Hakim fucked me, he asked what it felt like to

be fucked by the Holy Spirit," she said, her voice sweet. "He would bend my legs under me and yell at me, 'Fuck me, your African black man. Fuck your big-dick nigger. Fuck your God.'"

Jean raised her head and looked into his eyes. She seemed moved by his compassionate face, his sincerity, and his caring smile. He lay quietly beside her and spoke to her softly.

She started to weep, the sobs building to a crescendo as if all was lost. "My baby. My baby. My baby," she moaned.

He held her tightly, his arms wrapped around her as she sat up. The tears soaked through his shirt, wetting the fabric.

He hadn't imagined this. That she was still messed up by the poisonous memory of Hakim and the nightmarish episode of her dead baby. He stopped in mid-motion, his hand up in the air, and she turned to face him. No words had to be spoken. The moment of desire had passed, vanished like vapor, like cigarette smoke. They knew what had just happened. They knew they couldn't go through with it.

She crawled off the bed, went to the bathroom and dressed hurriedly. He waited for her to finish. When she came back, they hugged very close, almost like lovers in love.

Then, she left, closing the door gently behind her. He never saw her alive again.

III. Mayhem

Someone said Jean had one nervous breakdown after another, having to be hospitalized on numerous occasions. She was overcome by paranoia and grief, with severe bouts of depression. She continued to work in Europe although her movie roles in Hollywood were far fewer. He talked to her during this time, but they could not get together. Maybe Jean wanted it that way.

Every anniversary of her stillborn baby's birth, she tried to kill herself. The year before her end, Jean survived an attempt where she threw herself under a train on the Paris Metro. Passengers pulled her to safety. She was hospitalized after the incident, supposedly to prevent her from doing harm to herself

Her final call came for him a couple of days before she was scheduled to work on a new film, *La Legion Saute sur Kolnezzi*, with Georges de Beauregard, the producer of Godard's *Breathless*. She sounded like old Jean, joking and laughing. He didn't detect anything wrong. However, there were other calls, where the actress was confused, somewhat distraught, even incoherent. Sometimes, she needed consolation. Sometimes, she needed stability, breaking sentences in two, jumping from one idea to another.

Once, in a drunken rage, she recited the words from a leaked press clipping about the two-toned baby written by columnist Joyce Haber from the *LA Times*: "Meanwhile, the outgoing Miss A. was pursuing several free-spirited causes, among them the black revolution. She lived in a way she believed raised a few Establishment eyebrows. Not because her escorts were often blacks, but because they were black nationalists. And now, according to all those really "in" international sources, Topic A is the baby Miss A. is expecting and its father. Papa's said to be a rather prominent Black Panther."

At other times, Jean talked about Clint Eastwood, saying what a nice man he was and speaking of his love of jazz. She told him about Belmundo and his many moods. She was drinking heavily. Frequently, she railed against Otto Preminger—his insincerity, his affairs with his stars, including Dorothy Dandridge. She said he'd sold her to Columbia which didn't know how to use her.

"Otto was a bastard," she mumbled. "He threatened to replace me with Audrey Hepburn on the film, *Bonjour Tristesse*. He sold me like a slave."

Mostly, during these conversations, he just listened, letting her talk.

Jean cried, sad over her ex-husband, Romain. "I miss him. He was a lover and friend. He was the only one who understood me." He'd stood by her during the furor over the race of the baby. She told Salim about a group of American white women who called her "a nigger-loving white bitch" while one of them spat on her. Romain would later shoot and kill himself, a year after Jean's death.

Her calls stopped three weeks before her death. He knew something had happened. After the actress married Dennis Berry, the son of director John Berry, in 1971, she took up with Ahmed Hasmi, although she was not divorced from Berry. Jean was missing for eleven days before she was discovered in the back seat of a car, wrapped in a blanket, in a suburb of Paris. The police said she died from an overdose of barbiturates. But in 1980, the Paris press hinted that Jean's death might not be a suicide, that she had been drinking, and that her body showed an "extraordinarily high level of alcohol". The papers suggested someone had placed her in the car while she was alive and comatose.

How easy it would have been for three or four FBI men to grab Jean, pin her in a chair, bind her arms, and force her mouth open to pop the pills and pour down the booze. How had they forced her to write a suicide note? Maybe under the fear of death.

The note, left for her son, read: "I can't deal with a world that beats the weak, puts down the blacks and women, and massacres infants."

Remembering their time together, Salim didn't know whether the feds got her, or the enveloping fog of sadness swallowed her, he only knew it hurt his heart thinking of her final, dark moments.

Salim attended the service for Jean. Her three former husbands and her last lover, Hasmi, stood around the grave site. There was a sizable crowd along with a platoon of French photographers. Someone read a poem she had written as a teenager: "I went through the woods for a walk in the rain, and as I walked, my soul was freed from pain."

After, in the cab, Salim sobbed like a disappointed child, a worse grief than the celestial farewell for Fred Hampton. He reminded himself that Jean was at peace. *Jean is at peace. Jean is at peace.* The cabbie turned to him and offered him a tissue. It started to drizzle as if on cue.

It's Tight Like That

It was after three in the morning when the show was over. We packed up our instruments, content that we had done our best, earned our bread. The owner of the Club Sublime, a speakeasy on the city's swanky shore, invited us back to his penthouse place overlooking the ships and the glittering lake. We knew better than to refuse his offer. Flanked by his gunmen, he told us he had some people over there and that we could pick up some more cash if we stuck around.

One of Mr. Danton's bodyguards, his gun in plain view, slung a girl into our sedan, a female with the coloring of chocolate milk. She smiled at me and started going through her purse. The hood shoved two more girls on top of us, cursed at them, and slammed the door.

It was hot as hell. The kind of heat that made your skin stick to your clothes. I was burning up. I kept coughing, coughing, coughing. Everybody looked at me like I had TB, like I was going to cough up a lung.

"You awight?" the chocolate girl asked. She had a bowl haircut, almost mannish, but it fit her looks.

"No, I'm okay, smoke too damn much," I answered her.

The other girls didn't seem convinced, casting me strange glances. All the dames wore the customary chorus girl outfits, tight in all the right places, but the chocolate girl had slipped into a man's pinstriped suit, starched white collar, and black crook's shoes. She toyed around with a thick, stinky cigar. Puffed on it like a burly dockworker.

Her man worked for Capone. The thin man with a beak nose was involved in every felonious activity imaginable: gun smuggling, bootlegging liquor, gambling, whores, and speakeasies. After the 1923 election of the Mayor, Bill Dever, everything changed. Capone and his boys moved into Cicero, making it their turf, and doing battle with local gangster Myles O' Donnell. The skirmish cost over 200 lives.

"Bitch has too much rouge on," Mr. Danton said. He didn't make anything of her dressing in guy's clothes. He must have liked it.

"Yes," I replied. I didn't like the mobster, but I knew better than to get on his bad side.

Mr. Danton, like Capone, had other things on his mind. Their rivals, the gang from the North Side, was trying to muscle into their turf. Bugs Moran and Hymie Weiss had shot up the restaurant at the Lexington Hotel where Capone and his boys hung out. A gang of cars, with hoods using Thompson sub-machine guns and shotguns, attacked the hotel and the restaurant. Many people were hurt. Following that ruckus, Capone ordered several armored Cadillacs with bullet-proof windows for his favored men. Mr. Danton had one and used it to go between nightspots.

"How about going over to Inky's spot?" the mobster asked. "How about it, girls?" His voice didn't go with his body. It was shrill, high-pitched, and utterly feminine. He was a pug-ugly bastard too.

The girls nodded submissively. Only the chocolate one

sneered and folded her arms. The mobster noticed the gesture and slapped her viciously. She took it.

"You come too, Viv," Mr. Danton growled, trembling with visible rage. His eyes narrowed into slits.

In her man's suit, possibly wearing his drawers, she looked like a ripe fruit. She made a bored face and rolled her eyes as she puffed the stinky stogie.

"I own you, body and soul," he said.

Later, when we got to Inky's place, I got her alone. Her hands were shaky. She told me she was scared of them, especially him. We shared a drink and a reefer stick before she went into a back room.

"Look at me. I'm a real sinner." She chuckled. "The daughter of a fire-and-brimstone preacher. I'm sleepin' with evil."

"You got to sort it out," I said. "Your life is totally confused." I knew she was a good girl, deep underneath the surface.

"I'm scared of mens, all mens," Viv said, as she made her exit after changing hurriedly into her vixen garb. "Do you know what I mean? He makes me do things," she whispered, as if he could hear her all the way across town. "He makes me lick his wife and her sister. Then they sat up and drink cocktails and watch him fuck me. That's they damn entertainment."

"Damn," I muttered.

"I feel safe with you." She grinned.

"You shouldn't," I retorted. "Like you said, I'm just like all the rest. Remember, I am a man too. I will disappoint you."

"I need you," she moaned and shivered. Dragged on the reefer quickly.

I held her. Her slender arms went about me tightly, her body pressing against me, and I felt her crying. I kissed her tenderly, stroking her hair.

She stuck her thumb in her mouth. She always had to have something between her lips, something to comfort her. A thumb or a stiff pee-wee. Just a once-innocent country girl corrupted by the Big City. Out of her depth.

At the rehearsals, while Lil, Satchmo's wife, was suffering from a bad chest cold, he let me sit in and play her parts. The boys who he was going to make the record with were all here: Kid Ory on trombone, Johnny Dodds on clarinet, Johnny St. Cyr on banjo, and myself on the ivories.

We did some of what the trumpet man planned for us to do, a little bit of *Dippermouth Blues*, *Just Gone*, *Mabel's Dream*, and a good deal of *Canal Street Blues*. I had trouble following these guys on that hopping *Canal Street* number. They chased me up and down the song until I got tired.

Satchmo laughed and laughed. Between numbers, Satchmo grinned. "I love to eat. Do you like chitlins?"

I shook my head.

"What about smoky short ribs and rice," he asked. "Fried okra, turned out shrimps, cornbread, collard greens, and sweet potatoes?"

"That's all right."

"You sound like a big-timer." He tinkered with a few light notes. "Yessuh, that's McKinney Cotton Pickers kind of grub."

He called me The Professor, maybe 'cause I had bright skin. Kinda light colored. Yella. He didn't usually favor light-complexion folks, but with me, he made an exception. He always stressed doing the right things.

Satchmo fingered the keys. "Professor, your mind can play tricks on you," he said, with that growl of his. "It can lie to you.

It can betray you. Your mind will tell you that you are a failure. That you're no good. Play no 'tention to it."

I let my fingers walk across the keys in a mocking tone. He knew I feared failure. I knew failure was tough. It would knock you on your ass.

"Failure is important to success," Satchmo suggested. "You got to fall down before you get back up. Or something like that."

My father, a house painter by trade and cornet player by night, had told me I was a failure. A loser. His people came down from Tutwiler, Mississippi. He'd said I was a big failure who didn't want to roll up his sleeves and tackle life.

Satchmo slurred a low bottom line. "Lemme tell you, Professor. Getting knocked down means you can look at the real man. All his parts. When that happens, don't lie to yourself. Don't pretend you're something you're not."

Kid Ory cut me a new butt hole for playing the same solo note for note. He called me last. "No juice. None of that cakewalk music or ragtime," he shouted.

Satchmo nodded because he was right. See, ole Satchelmouth could remember phrases from songs and ditties back from the old days. "Don't forget the ham bones," he snickered. "Or crawfish."

Suddenly, he brought the horn to his lips and took flight. The notes hung in the soft air above the crowd like blue jays riding the currents of wind. We were stunned, but then nobody had ever heard a trumpet played like that. This was new. He toyed with the valves, producing a sound like the blood-red moon, the high hips of a warm chippie, the cold lines of sad tears. Slur, smear, triplet. Arpeggios, grace notes, slow or rocking. Always full of feeling.

"You dig, Professor?" he rasped.

There was a tradition of folks who played this music. Hippolyte Charles, Sam Morgan, Kid Rena, Punch Miller, Willie Coke, Leslie Dimes, Walter Blue. Like me, they had played all over, riverboats, circuses, vaudeville shows, roadhouses, juke joints, even funerals. I wasn't a big fan of dying. Rather than work a funeral one time, I went to work on a cane harvest.

"Take it on the downbeat," Kid said, holding his licorice stick.

"Easy Papa," Satchmo said.

I used to dream about coming to Chicago or New York. With Satchmo, this was possible. He was a first-class showman. A teacher and father to us all. He didn't remind white folks that his life was not that easy when he was a kid. And sometimes, he would clown and do that darkie jive. But all of us knew what he was doing. Jim Crow was still on the throne. My great-aunt used to call Satchmo's routine "playing the fool".

He was a whole man, not a jester or a clown. He told me that a peckerwood asked him if the blues reminded him of dying and death. The Great Man said everybody thinks about dying some time but the blues ain't about that. The blues was about getting the thorns, the pain, and suffering of life. He explained nobody gone live forever and the white man had shot back that nobody had come back from the other side.

Satchmo roared with laughter and said you just live as long as you can. Love life, and let life love you.

The blues were here in this country before we were born.

Like Satchmo, I was partial to brown and chocolate women. He teased me because I had a chocolate gal. Skin color was important in the South. And Viv's skin had that sheen to it. He didn't trust Viv, but he didn't tell me why.

Viv would always say, "I got a battalion of mens falling all over themselves to get me, falling on they knees, bringing diamonds and flowers, proposing and asking me for my hand with they dicks out."

Sometimes I stalked her, followed her around. I once watched her quietly in her room, without her knowing it. She was talking dirty to the mobster under a bare light bulb with a red scarf on it. Her middle fingers, wet and glistening, were jammed deep in her sex. Her sweating face lolled back in obvious ecstasy. Her pussy scent hung thick in the air like candle smoke. She must have been stoking her cat for a long time before the mobster straddled her and brought her pouting lips to his hard bone. I was finished with her at that moment.

We finished the gig over at The Tulip and went over to The Hot Clam Club, which was swankier and high class. Tuxes and top hats. You could hear our echo walking through the long corridors of the place. Four servants, burly white guys costumed like overdressed clowns, stood guard. The customers and gamblers were milling around the premises, looking from room to room, seeing the crazy sights. It was a freak show.

One or two of the girls walked between rooms, jumping into action, adding a little spice. They wore silk robes as they switched their asses through the hallways. Everybody looked at them. I wondered if Viv was in all that hell.

I carried a set of drumsticks. The last thing some of these whites would accept was a colored man wandering around in the club, big as you please, without any good reason to be there, so I used the old trick used by my elders. Musicians are harmless. Maybe I should have taken up the banjo.

A gal with big titties walked through the white crowd, twitching like a female in heat. Everything jiggling and bouncing.

Especially her round, wide ass. She hummed something.

"Ah stay nice brown all year round," she sang. "Member that."

I waded through them. The girls, now in greater number, moved like the undead, like zombies, floating like feathers through the men as if they were sleepwalking. Shadowy figures. Often the girls screamed and giggled like silly schoolgirls, and the mobsters felt them up, slipping into another room.

A crowd gathered in the doorway of one room. All the men were talking, drinking, laughing. It was a free and easy mood. I peeked inside, and there was a woman alone on top of a table, with her breasts out and a short, black skirt showing off flashes of her sex and butt cheeks. She flirted with the men who pounded on the long table in a wild native rhythm, squeezing her breasts as she wiggled and let the building music take over her flesh. All eyes were on her every twist and bump.

They yelled and hollered like something crazy. She rolled her hips, her hands running up and down her thighs and long legs. Hot blood seemed to course through her veins like a drum beat in an African rhythm. These men came to see her. They were her friends. Her lovers. At least that was the way they acted. The men could see everything under her skirt and yelled rudely. Each man locked eyes on her, and when she did a low bow where her business could be advertised, I grabbed her by the arm and dragged her off the table. We ran and ran. Her customers must have been so mad at me.

"Will you do me a favor?" Viv said. "Don't worry about me anymore. I'm a big girl."

I shook my head. "Somebody needs to worry about you."

"Nobody worries about Viv. Nobody," she said. "When I was thirteen, I was raped by a man who roomed with my folks.

He held a knife to my throat. He pulled me off into the woods where there was another man. They kept the knife at my neck as they took turns on me."

"Oh damn."

"One of them wanted to cut me," she said, her voice low and sad. "He sliced the knife 'cross the soft part of my upper thigh. The tender part. The cut was very deep and made a bad scar."

"I felt it when we loved," he replied.

"How did you like the free show?" the girl asked. "I had them under control. They was eating out of my hand."

"That's crazy." I frowned. "Are you afraid of crooks?"

"No."

"I don't like them using you like that. Like a toy. Like a cheap whore. You deserve better than that. You know that."

"Don't you turn out to be a creep like the others." There was a warning in her look. "These mens often confuse lust and love in a way gals don't. They can't separate sex and love like gals do. Most of these boys have some good sex with a woman and fall in love with her."

He grimaced. "Don't you trust me?"

"You're pathetic, just like the others." She laughed sweetly and walked toward the maid's room. She closed the door gently behind her.

I followed, and she dropped to her knees and unzipped my pants. I felt the warmth of her mouth on me.

She sucked both balls into her mouth, cupped them, and licked me between my legs.

She laughed that special laugh of hers, that girlish giggle.

Whispering sweetly in her ear, I opened her up with my fingers and slid down to kiss her belly and then run my moist tongue along the crease to her button. She whimpered and put her hands up to crush my mouth against her pussy. I sucked and lapped at her juicy sex. She gasped as my tongue snaked inside her, in and out slowly. I tongue-fucked her until her legs trembled. Her pelvis ground against my mouth, hotly and savagely, while I licked her deeper.

I could see she was close. My fingers were up in her, curling, fondling the thick lips of her sex. Now, her button was between my teeth, swollen to its peak, and my tongue darted across it again and again and again. Her back arched as she screamed, cumming in my mouth.

Satchmo sat in over at the Tulip, his trumpet under his arm. The folks looked happy to have him in the place. We rocked the club, the mobsters laughing and patting the chorus girls on their backsides, and the horn man doing his King Oliver thing by winking and grinning, "Hotter than a forty-five."

When we joked around during the show, the owners liked it because everything was free and easy. The customers loved it and ordered more drinks. They liked having Satchmo around; his smile and his gravel voice made the people happy. He was a whole man, not a jester or a clown. I really thought that.

I was playing behind him, with his greatness on full display, that brass tone bold and swaggering and manly. It was a tone which warmed and penetrated the spirit. We would listen to him, his mastery of ideas, turning and twisting the melody. He would really have his way with a song. Every night was a blowing session with everybody getting a chance to solo.

He knew what the customers wanted, and he let you make mistakes because he knew that was the only way you could grow. He talked to you when you needed his counsel.

Some of the white players sneaked into the place and started writing down the solos and stealing solos. He didn't care. Satchmo smiled at me and joked about them getting a good education from "dese cullud boys."

The trombonist did a two-step, snapping fingers. "Do it, boy!"

The Gut-Bucket Blues. The Sportin' Girl Gone Bad Blues. The Zulu Blues. The Sharecropper Blues. It all reminded me of the time the Navy closed Storyville down because of the women and hot sex. They emptied out the cribs of baby dolls, pimps, and the strong-arm cullud boys who'd brought it on themselves by robbing and killing the sailors. Gone was old Lulu White's place.

"You's a mess, Professor," Satchmo said. "You worried about that sporting gal. She gone git you killed."

"I love her," I mumbled. "I know she ain't no good."

Satchmo roared. "You got it real bad. I had a yen for one of them gals once, a Creole gal, Daisy Parker. Oh, baby, I would have done anything to get with that gal. She had my nose open real bad. I guess you got it like I had it for Daisy."

With the last song, he leaned back and reached those blazing, otherworldly high notes. When the clapping quieted, he bent over and aimed the horn at the floor. After it was over, he led me back to the dressing room, shoved a bunch of jack into my hand and pushed me out of the door. Outside, the dark was thick in the alley. And soon, the headlights of a car momentarily blinded me as it pulled to a stop.

The car door opened. I saw fear in her eyes as she wiggled around on the seat, two suitcases at her feet. There were tears in her eyes.

"Where are we going?"

"Nowhere in particular but any place away from here," she said.

I scooted in next to her. "We will disappear, vanish. Into shadow."

This was Satchmo's gift to me. A Storyville valentine.

Mr. Robeson at The Moment

The government had me over a barrel. They had the goods on me and wanted me to do something that I hated doing. Let me explain myself fully. I'm a New York City politician, a colored one. A district boss in a way. Sometimes power goes straight to your head, especially when you come from modest beginnings. You get a taste of the High Life, and you never want it to leave your mouth. The government made a deal with me. If I did this favor for them, then all my past mistakes would go away. All of them. I didn't know how they were going to do that, but I didn't ask any questions.

What happened was one of my so-called pals ratted me out to the Feds, said I was trying to bribe my way into a third term as state senator. I always thought Adam Clayton Powell had something to do with this, but I couldn't prove it.

One of the honchos from the state Democratic machine said to the press, "With the mounting allegations of corruption against Senator Fast, we believe he should consider whether he can properly serve his constituents."

This stoolie, like some of the old guard from the party, got my endorsement and campaign help when he was running for public office. But now they have all turned on me. This all started six months ago when three government agents visited me at my office in Albany and presented me with their plan. They said they could get an indictment by a grand jury, and I could face up to 35 years in prison. I couldn't believe it. I couldn't believe my so-called political pals could roll over on me like that. Even my former wife furnished them with information of a confidential nature.

"We have the evidence against you, with one of your cronies swearing he set up meetings with party leaders and prominent businessmen and negotiated thousands of dollars in bribes," one of the Feds said, looking stern.

"Who said this?" I said angrily. "Who told this lie?"

"We're not going to tell you that," another Fed replied.

The other agent scribbled notes. "This man says he pocketed $30,000 for his work. We've got you dead to rights. He led us to all of the gentlemen who were involved in this scheme and most of them are starting to talk."

"State Senator Fast, I don't understand you," the first agent said. "You've had a long, honorable career in public service. You've had your glory days. You stood for something. The voters looked up to you. Why would you do this?"

As I faced them across the desk, I questioned my reasoning for joining in this scheme. Why would I risk everything to wallow in this mud? Why would I get hooked up with these guys who were crooks and charlatans? I'd gotten desperate. I was slipping in popularity in my district. There was so much irony here. Because I did this stupid thing, everybody was running for the hills.

"They say you colored lack a certain sense of character, is that true?" the first agent asked while the others glared at me.

"I don't know about that," I said, still defiant.

"I think it's the power and greed." He smirked. "I think

corruption is rampant among you guys. You all have been there too long. That's what happens. The people should throw you bums out and elect better candidates. You knew the law. You messed up."

I sat down and lit a cigarette. "I won't quit."

That was when the trio of them began laughing, laughing so hard that they were holding their sides. I didn't like where this situation was going. I didn't like their laughter.

"Is this all the corruption you were involved in?" the second man asked. "Maybe there are other things out there, worse things."

I blew out smoke and snarled. "There aren't any other things."

"Do we throw the book at you, or do you cooperate?" the first agent asked. "Maybe you can avoid all of this trouble. Maybe we can make it all go away. But we need something from you."

"I'm not quitting," I said. Frowning, I stubbed my cigarette out in the ashtray. "The people in my district need me."

The first man walked around the desk and jerked me up by the arm, wrinkling my suit jacket. "None of this has been made public, but one call to the prosecutor's office, and that's it for you. You're a damn liar and a thief. You don't deserve the public's trust."

I stood toe-to-toe with him, smelling the stench of a vendor's frankfurter, mustard, and stale beer. "I'll make myself clear. I am not quitting. You cannot strong-arm me. You cannot make me do what you want me to do."

The agent smiled and shoved me back into the seat. "Do you think the voters in your district will want to vote for you again after we reveal the dirt you have done over the years? Nobody wants to be played for a fool."

"What did my office manager say about me?" I wanted to know if my inner circle was loyal to me.

"It seems Mr. Webb doesn't really like you," the second man piped up. "He thinks you're too damn intense, too wound up. He thinks you're hard on the help, asking them to go the extra mile. He says there has been a lot of turn-over in your office with people getting fed up and feeling it's not worth the effort. He thinks you're a real bastard."

The first agent hinted that the secretaries in the main office were even more unflattering about me. They said I talked down to my staff and lowered the boom on workers when I had a bad day.

"That's a bald-faced lie," I retorted. "I'm not like that."

The first agent sat on the corner of my desk and whispered to me about agents questioning the other legislators about my legislative performance and possible illegalities in funding of community groups during my last campaign. He added that there were some issues about my use of public funds for several nonprofit organizations.

"You're on a fishing expedition," I replied. "You'll find nothing there. Every time a Negro tries to do something good and positive, you guys try to swat him down. You know I don't tolerate corruption of any sort! Of any sort!"

All three agents circled me and gave me a long, hard look. They all wore gray suits, crew-cuts, and the same sour expressions on their pale faces.

"Do you know Paul Robeson?" the first agent asked.

"Sure, I know him. Everybody knows him. He's a famous man. The biggest Negro man in the world. Why do you ask?"

The agent handed me a thick file folder. "You know Mr. Robeson, the entertainer and activist. The government knows you know him because you have attended some of his concerts and speeches. We've had him under surveillance for a long time. Mr. Robeson says he's not a commie, a Red, but he visited Russia back in the 1930s. He has many friends who are fellow travelers, and he's always appearing at socialist meetings and conferences. He's fascinated by the enemies of America and democracy."

The second agent pulled up a chair and recited the party line. "Mr. Robeson's often quoted in *The Daily Worker* and other commie rags. Now, this is what he said about Russians who didn't go along with Stalin's program: 'From what I have already seen of the workings of the Soviet government, I can only say that anybody who lifts his hand against it ought to be shot.' These are not the words of someone who loves this country."

I glared at them and frowned. "All I know is that Mr. Robeson is against the colonization of Africa and has thrown his support behind the blacks there. That's a good thing."

"Did you know he had his son educated in Moscow?" the first agent asked.

I shook my head. "No."

"Did you know he worshipped Stalin, the commie tyrant who killed millions of his people?" he asked. "Mr. Robeson got the 1952 Stalin Peace Prize. He called Stalin a man with deep humanity, wise and good. Stalin was a killer, a cold-blooded killer. Mr. Robeson is politically naive."

I smiled. "Maybe he was duped by the Russians."

The agents laughed. "You understand little about how the world operates politically. A real babe in the woods, right?" one of them said.

A sly laugh came from the agent standing near the door.

"Even Jackie Robinson, a hero to your people, distanced himself from Mr. Robeson before the House Committee on Un-American Activities because Robeson was a commie and loved the Russians more than he did America. Jackie Robinson was a patriot and loved this country."

"Some people in my community considered Robinson a snitch and a sellout," I said, countering his statement.

"Negroes are naive," the first agent said. "They don't know when this government is looking out for them. I know this much. They should not consider Mr. Robeson to be one of their leaders. He is a dead-end."

"What do you mean by that?" I wondered what he was getting at. Were they going to kill Mr. Robeson?

Now, the first agent was all smiles. "We want you to befriend Mr. Robeson. Find out all his habits. Find out the identities of his associates, both in and out of the communist party. Find out his schedule. Get as close as you can."

I shook my head. "No, no, no."

"Or the story of your dirty deeds will be splashed all over the papers," the second man said. He sneered. "You won't be elected as dog catcher. And you will probably see some time behind bars. We're not fucking around with you. You do this thing, or you go down."

I continued shaking my head. I couldn't do it. I couldn't rat out Mr. Robeson, a man who I respected and admired. They'd made it plain; it was him or me.

"We're confident you'll make the right decision." Just as quickly as they appeared on my doorstep, they disappeared. They would call me a week from Tuesday to get my decision, one of them said as they headed out the door.

After the agents left, I sat in the empty office, staring at the damn folder, wondering what I would do. I lit a cigarette, walked to the window which had a panoramic view of New York's capital city. All my friends in the party were deserting me, heading for the hills, in light of the rumor of ethics violations about to be made public. Nothing was secret in this town. Maybe I could make a deal with some of the senior state party leaders, make nice, and beg their forgiveness. Maybe then they would guarantee a fair process and not throw the book at me.

I couldn't believe someone would snitch on me. All the damn good I've done for the state, all the favors I've done, and now they want to send me to jail. It didn't seem real.

"The government wants me to go to prison," I said, but there was no reply from the empty room. They'd targeted me because of my race. They never want any of us to have political power.

I called my brother, James, an attorney, and spilled everything that had happened to me that day. My voice was shrill, almost hysterical. I was scared. My shirt was soaked with my nervous sweat. "James, I really messed up this time," I sobbed.

My brother's words sobered me up. "Your wife said she's going to the cops. Said you beat and choked her. Is that true?"

"My ex-wife," I reminded him. "She's lying." Anger made my voice tight.

"Ruth is still your wife by law," he countered. "You haven't got a divorce decree. She came to our home because she knows what trouble you're in, and she doesn't want to make it worse. And, you know, she could do just that."

I didn't want to talk about my wife; I wanted to talk about my stalled political career. "She left me, Jimmy. I didn't leave her."

"She left because you work all the time," my brother retorted.

"She left because you're never home. When you are there, you fight over money, bills, car notes, everything. She said you were drunk and punched her in the face, kicked her in the stomach, and choked her until she almost fainted."

I was mad that she would go to someone outside our home to blab our private affairs. "Ruth is lying. She makes shit up. I'd never strike my wife, never. I've done a lot of bad things, but I'd never hit my wife."

My brother said I should get my family matters together before the law got into the act. He also told me if Ruth wanted to go to the police, it would not go well for me. I agreed with him about that.

"But what about this other mess I'm facing, Jimmy?" I wanted to scream at him that I had thrown in the towel. I was weak. I was corrupt, and I expected to pay for everything I'd done and, possibly, a few things I hadn't.

"You got yourself into this shit; you get yourself out," my brother replied. "Your mouth wrote a check that your ass can't cash. I can't believe that you didn't know this would happen."

"No, I didn't realize anything." I hung up the phone, walked to the center of the room and screamed for about two minutes. I didn't know how I could survive this mess.

Five days later, I decided how I would play along with their game. I'd give them nothing. My mind was full of Robeson facts, little details of his habits and obsessions, the delicious family stuff, his bold political views, and his true convictions that he could make the world a better place. When I was ready, I had my assistant call his people to set up a meeting.

On a Thursday, we met the apartment of his friend, a guy he'd known since his salad days. The place was near Park Avenue and Forty-Sixth Street. I came alone, without an entourage.

The place was very comfortable, lived-in, and full of expensive furniture. I wondered how they controlled their children, a girl and two boys under the age of ten. The government's prey must have known the agency would go after him with one of his own. Another cullud boy. However, Robeson was no fool and would never let anybody get too close to his business or his family. He was much too smart for any plan directly taking him on.

A Latin man, possibly a Puerto Rican fellow traveler in a finely-tailored brown suit, stood near the entrance of the living room, intentionally blocking any view of Robeson. I heard movement from the other room, the radio's volume increasing, and then his booming, bass voice. It was only fitting that I would hear the power of his voice before I laid eyes on him. The government had rehearsed me what to say. I only acted the part.

"Mr. Robeson will be right out," another man, balding and neatly dressed, said as he passed near me. "He says he remembers you. You made quite an impression."

I found a seat on a couch that was the same color as the drapes. Canary-yellow. That must have been the wife's style influence; no man would choose such a color. Too loud, too bright, too bold. I wanted to smoke but fought down the urge. There were no family noises. No kids running and yelling or wifely comments coming from the back rooms.

Suddenly, there was he was, walking regally and purposeful toward me. Mr. Paul Robeson. The target. He formally shook my hand, but a pat on the arm made a less rigid gesture. I felt I was among friends. However, he wanted to get right to the point. I hated being rushed yet I knew his time was knotted up in a tight schedule.

"Mr. Fast, what do you need?" Mr. Robeson asked.

"I think you're jumping the gun," I answered. "I just wanted to ask your advice on a matter. I didn't want any kind of promise or endorsement."

"When a politician like yourself comes a-calling, there must be something you need," he said. "I read something about you in the paper. You're in trouble, but nothing is sticking. I can't be any help to you. I've got trouble up to here." His gaze seemed to search my face like he tried to read my mind to find out why I was there.

People with his kind of fame had to be careful who they mingled with in their inner circle. But if I gave the government what they wanted, everything would be cleared up they'd said. I was torn.

"So now they're using some of my own people to try and spy on me," the entertainer said, staring at me. "This will not be the first time. I didn't mind when Jackie Robinson came to Washington to speak before the HUAC. We're friends. We know how the game is played."

"What are you saying, Mr. Robeson?"

His slight smile made me think he liked when I addressed him formally. It probably made him feel important.

"You know why they don't like me, State Senator Fast?" Mr. Robeson asked. He smirked. "They want me to go on my knees before them. That won't happen. It never will."

I leaned back on the soft, comfortable cushions of the couch. "I don't know. The government has a way of getting its way. I've learned not to underestimate it. I have a healthy respect for how it runs."

Mr. Robeson stood and whispered something to the man standing at the door, who disappeared. We continued talking, with the rebel-rouser holding the floor, speaking again in that melodic voice.

"Mr. Fast, I answer my critics when they say I act superior or arrogant. Too much like a white man, by explaining how a man must hold himself to a certain set of standards, no matter who that man is. When I was at Rutgers, during the first few weeks of football practice, these white gentlemen, some players, intentionally injured me."

I didn't know anything about that. That had not been in the file folder. I nodded like I was following him closely so he would continue.

"What did they do?" I asked.

He moved his nose with his fingers. "They broke my nose and dislocated my shoulders. I still feel that bad shoulder even today."

I shook my head. "Why?"

"Why do you think they did it? They hated the sight of me. After I returned to practice, I went back to the team. I never thought of quitting. I couldn't do it. The hate continued. Another guy stepped on my hand with his sharp cleats. Hurt like hell."

"What did you do?"

He smiled broadly and then laughed. "On the next play, I grabbed that same guy, who was running with the ball, and I lifted him high over my head. I thought about slamming him hard to the ground, but the coach shouted at me to put him down. And I did. But nobody messed with me after that."

"So, what is the point of your story, Mr. Robeson?"

He folded his massive arms, grinned, and fixed his eyes with a determined gaze. "Expect no quarter. Expect no mercy. The enemy is not content to simply defeat you; the enemy wants to destroy you as well."

I thought of my own government problems. "I know that too well."

Mr. Robeson ducked his head into another room, saying something to someone there in a whisper. When he returned to me, he said, "Senator Fast, as my folks used to say to me, never take low. Stand your ground and hit them back harder. Never cower. Never beg or plead."

"It doesn't do any good," I disagreed. He could not be anyone's hero.

"I met President Truman to ask him if he could do something about lynching," the activist said. "Maybe he could pass legislation with teeth in it to stop them. It was happening almost every other week. Truman quickly ended the meeting and left."

"You're too outspoken," I murmured. "I don't talk too much. I never talk out of turn. Or too boldly."

"You won't score points like that," Mr. Robeson said. "You must speak up. You must let them know you exist. You must let them know there is still more fight in you."

I slumped over. "I'm whipped. I can't fight them anymore."

"You've got to fight, got to fight," he answered with a bite to his words. "My father was a slave, and people like him helped build this country. People like him took a lot of insults and punishment to stay here. They can't force me to leave. They took my passport, but I always found a way. There was always someone to help me."

"They've got me in a corner, and nothing can help me," I whined. "Not even you. Nothing or nobody."

His voice seemed to boom, filling the air in the room. "Do you know the date of August 27, 1949? Does it have any significance for you?"

"Not really."

There was no anger or remorse on his face as he filled me in. "This was when the forces of evil tried to silence me, to quiet my message. The government moved against me on that date in Peekskill, New York. Nobody wants to talk about what happened in Peekskill."

"What happened?" I asked.

"Pete Seeger and I, along with some other entertainment people, were scheduled to appear in Peekskill, but there was some tension about whether the locals would allow us to perform," Robeson said. "The police assured us there would not be any trouble. But that was not the case. A large crowd, good American patriots, some wearing VFW and American Legion hats, surrounded the long line of cars, people who'd come to see the show. They jeered at them. Some were liquored up and rocked the cars, smashing the windows, screaming commie bastards, commie bitches! A few of them yelled nigger-lovers and kill the big darkie! This was not American democracy on full display!"

I felt ashamed of myself, not able to look at his powerful face. Why was I there? Why would I agree to something like this?

"You must remember, Senator Fast, these were good, hard-working people just wanting to attend a show with some great speeches and excellent singing," Mr. Robeson said, his voice bottomless. "All they got was the hell scared out of them. I was so angry at the people who were supposed to protect the concertgoers. They threatened them, saying once they got inside, they would not get out alive. What is that? That is not justice or fair play."

"Did you try to go above the heads of the local authorities?"

I asked. I knew the answer before I asked the question.

"Calls to the state police fell on deaf ears," he said. "No help came."

The man standing near the door walked over to me. He was the kind of guy who could take care of himself if it was needed. "They wanted some trouble to break out," he said. "They wanted to let the mob attack the people attending the concert, so they could say the commies started everything."

Mr. Robeson sat in a straight-backed chair, frowning as he described the bloody Peekskill concert. "It was terror," he said, crossing his massive arms. "Nobody did anything to help us. They burned crosses on the hillside around the people, and the mob got more agitated by the minute, crowds of angry men attacking cars on the road leading to the picnic ground. There were buses full of boys and girls, mostly our race, who were there in the hollow surrounded by tall trees. The union members were determined not to let anything happen to those young souls. But those children heard the windshields of the cars being smashed, saw the crosses burning, and heard the taunts, and foul language as the hateful rock throwers and others with billy clubs got closer." His face twisted as he spoke of the painful memories.

"Where the hell were the cops? I really don't understand it."

"The police couldn't get to the women and children because an American Legion truck was pulled across the road, blocking everything. There were several battles between the union people and the concert goers with the mob, blood flowing on both sides. Finally, the law came with their guns drawn and told the mob they should take it easy, that they would break the concert up. Then they turned to the peaceful people, accusing them of being outside agitators, big city troublemakers with their commie sympathizers."

Embarrassed by my Judas mission, I didn't want to hear any more of his Peekskill story. All I wanted was to get out of there.

"Shortly after that, a melee broke out, and they got the better of the concert goers," Mr. Robeson continued. "They bloodied everyone who stood in their way while the police stood there, doing nothing. Women ran to the protection of the youngsters in the hollow, dresses torn, faces battered and bruised. Some of the teen organizers had their eyes blackened, and mouths busted. My assistant carried a union organizer who had his head bashed open with a club, a deep wound in his scalp, blood gushing down his face. The organizers were scared for the gathering of women and little children, scared for the rush of goons hurling bottles and rocks at the precious huddled group at the center of the hollow. The attackers yelled they wanted to lynch me. Give us Robeson, give us the big nigger, they shouted."

He went on, pain and a deadly seriousness in his eyes. "You can imagine the screaming and shouting of the mob, but the organizers held firm, forming three barriers before the women and children, linking arms against the crazed mob, against their rocks and clubs. Many went down from the blows and injuries, but as soon as one fell, another would take his place. They fought mightily, bravely, boldly."

I almost wept. His words painted a courageous picture of warriors defending the honor and lives of the helpless and the innocent.

"Mr. Fast, do you know what they sang during the battle?" he asked.

I shook my head. I wanted to cover my face in shame.

His rich, baritone voice sang out, needing no accompaniment

or embellishment as he caressed the lyrics of an old hymn.

We shall not. We shall not be moved!
We shall not. We shall not be moved!
Just like a tree that's standing by the water,
we shall not be moved!

The man near the door seemed to sense my discomfort, sense that I wanted to leave, and moved closer to the doorway as if to make sure Mr. Robeson had the time to make his point. The singer talked about the hate and ignorance that reared their ugly heads that day in the face of the valiant people determined to make a stand. The symbol of the Peekskill tragedy resounded with a foul odor around the globe, he told me. He also said the concert was rescheduled for September 4th, but there were some dreadful incidents then too. Some 300 troopers stood guard, permitting them to go on with the show.

"I arrived about noon, demanding to go on despite warnings that there could be trouble again," Mr. Robeson said. "Pete Seeger went on before me, along with a pianist and some singers. Union people encircled the entire area, on alert. I walked out among the crowd, shaking hands, hugging those I knew. They didn't want me to sing for fear that I might be killed. I decided to sing regardless. I wanted to show those fascists that our cause was just. That we would not be silenced."

"Was there any trouble?" I asked.

He coughed deeply and continued. "Yes, as I said, there were some incidents, but I sang, and the people enjoyed it. When I was leaving in our car, the windshield was smashed, but we made it out safely."

I glanced at the man near the door, then at Robeson. "Why

did you tell me this dreadful story?"

He was practically staring right through me. I could imagine him using that same stare when he played Othello or Emperor Jones. "What is the worst they can do to you?" he asked.

"I don't want to think about that," I groaned.

"You played. Now, you got to pay," Mr. Robeson said sternly. "You cannot run with wolves and not expect to be eaten. You are associated with these people who could give a damn about you and your community and your future. Did you really expect them to be honest or treat you fairly?"

He was right. The political machine only fed off power and wealth, patronage and greed. How could I expect them to be merciful or have a conscience? I was just another victim, crushed under their mighty wheel.

"Take your punishment," Mr. Robeson said in that husky voice of his. He waved to someone in the other room. "My mail is opened, my phone is tapped, and I'm shadowed everywhere I go. Be a man. Don't be such a sissy. Take what's coming to you."

He asked the man to show me out. His expression said this meeting was over, that he couldn't help me, and that the government would win after all.

After they showed me out, I sat on a window sill in the entryway, pulled out a cigarette, and thought about getting out of town, leaving my family and my job behind. Mr. Robeson had only tried to counsel me, but everything he said only made me nervous. Very, very nervous.

Following the activist's words, I knew what I had to do. I called Greyhound and got a schedule to Chicago. Maybe I could get help there. As Mr. Robeson said, I would not take low. No sir.

Ask Her

I kept repeating this verse from the Bible, kept repeating it, kept repeating it, while on the train with a gun in my purse. "But many who are first shall be last, and the last shall be first." (Matthew 19:30).

My prayers don't get answered. I cannot get through. I cannot get through. Oh God, I cannot get through.

It was like when you called somebody, and it was busy. It has been busy for a long time. That busy signal, over and over. Please, God, I need somebody to talk to, before I do something foolish. Let one of my church friends call now. Please, please, please. Since I was from a pro-life family, a young soldier from the Christian right, I know my Bible backward and forward. My daddy, who is a soul warrior and an ordained minister, has fought against the cause of Roe v. Wade in several the Midwest states.

I've gone with him on these protests on the streets by the abortion mills where they butcher the young girls against their will. The slaughter of these babies demands justice. There must be justice for these criminals who cause the deaths of the unborn. The conscience of my soul cries out for these little spirits. I hear their painful cries in my head like the whining voice of the principal making lame announcements over the school PA system.

Sometimes I cried when I recited the Pledge of Allegiance. Tears just ran down my pink cheeks. I was overcome with love for my country.

"White girl, why you cryin' for?" asked one of the Negro girls.

"I just love my country and God so much," I replied. I hate that they won't let us recite The Lord's Prayer in school before we start our day. This was a culture of death, not love or salvation.

A while ago, we went to Florida to protest the case of Terri Schiavo, the sweet young martyr who was in a vegetative state and fed by a gastric tube. Her brain was not working; her cerebral cortex was ruined. We protested the fact that God's will would be done. We protested the fact that Congress, even the President, did not do anything to solve the family's agony. Everybody, who was among the faithful, wanted to let Terri's parents, Bob and Mary Schindler, take care of Terri. They knew the husband, Michael, was living with another woman. We knew that Terri should have been handed over to her caring parents. God must step into the mix when doctors can do no more. God controlled what Man cannot. God ruled who lives and who dies.

We prayed for Terri and her parents. We prayed for her when they let her die. God didn't like that decision. The Bible does not mention a living will, or that somebody must be artificially kept alive. It was a personal tragedy. God didn't turn his back on her. Man turned his back on Terri. The Congress should not have let her feeding tube be removed. Or the President. He is among the lost too.

This is the last time I'm going to think about evil. My parents say evil serves a purpose. Evil must be overwhelmed and not tolerated. Evil can be conquered. Daddy explains evil can be beaten by faith and righteousness and a deep understanding of human nature. He tells me evil demands our attention because we can't wrap our minds around it, and we must keep our urges in balance to maintain our lives in goodness. The sinister truth of America's future is that evil has embraced all the goodness and compassion found in most of us here. We have abandoned the teachings of God and Jesus. We have forsaken the word of the Holy Spirit. We are lost.

Please, someone, call me. Nobody saw me leave when I snuck out of the house, wearing black and carrying a gun in a gift-wrapped box. I have a mission for the Lord.

"The way of the wicked is an abomination unto the Lord, but he loveth him that followeth after righteousness." (Proverbs 15:9)

We are taught to be pro-life. For many women, abortion is a hobby. If you get knocked up, you make a call to Planned Parenthood and remove that life within your body. Or some confused girls take the abortion pill, RU-486, and flush the life right out of them down the toilet. My daddy told me how when Bill Clinton was the president, he removed all the rules of restrictions of counseling for young girls. He never protected the unborn. That's probably why he met such a sinful end to his term in White House.

"For the Lord knoweth the way of the righteous, but the way of the ungodly shall perish." (Psalm 1:6)

My daddy warns me about how young boys and men are evildoers. He says men always do foolish things that cripple their lives and happiness. Men are selfish. Men are flaky, weak, needy, controlling, immature, stupid, and untrustworthy. Only men who have been saved and bathed in the light of the Gospel are loving, caring, and protective of their women and their families. Other men try to change women for the worst. Daddy says many women stay in bad relationships out of duty, guilt, or obligation. He knows men and sinners.

"The heart is deceitful above all things and desperately wicked. Who knows it?" (Jeremiah 17:9)

Men, according to my papa, are a corrupting force. They are defenseless against their vices like drink, drugs, play, porn, and casual sex. Most men are addicted to sex. Their vanity lets them hurt girls and women to mask their hurt and torment. My daddy says a girl must consider her God-given purpose, her concerns, her needs. He explains that Christian men should protect their women. By joining their lives with hers, the men help them stay emotionally stable and safe.

"No man can serve two masters for either he will hate the one and love the other, or he will hold to one and despise the other. Ye cannot serve God and mammon." (Matthew 6:24)

Raymond told me he would love me forever. He lied. He moved his hand across my breasts, onto the soft flesh of my belly, and to the elastic of my white cotton panties. His broad fingers moved into the curly hair of my sex between my thighs, and he whispered that there was no one like me. He dipped his fingers into me, into my wetness as I wiggled against him. I remembered the Gospel and the words of my father, so insistent and demanding. But it felt so great with him touching me so. He mumbled into my ear that he would never hurt me as I heard the sound of the zipper of his pants.

"So shall it be at the end of the world. The angels shall come forth and sever the wicked from among the just. And shall cast them into the furnace of the fire. There shall be wailing and gnashing of teeth." (Matthew 13:49-50)

Daddy said to choose a man who values his worth in society as a husband and father and who would not be overwhelmed by the attractions of money, ambition, and arrogance. A man must treasure the role of a family man as pleasure and happiness and not just as a chore. A man must not resort to violence, vulgarity, and power to lord his control over his woman. Daddy says to remember that. Don't try to pick an ideal man, Daddy tells me.

"For we must all appear before the judgment seat of Christ that everyone may receive the things done in his body, according to that he hath done, whether it be good or bad." (II Corinthians 5:10)

For several weeks, I've suffered panic attacks, fourteen of them at last count. I don't know where they came from, maybe from something deep inside me. A few friends tried to tell me remedies for the attacks, but they keep coming back. I used to have these bouts of anxiety before reading a verse in Sunday school or when doing book reports in class. Daddy advised me to breathe deeply and try to exhale fully. I had one powerful panic attack before I stole the gun from Daddy's drawer.

"All we like sheep have gone astray. We have turned everyone to his own way, and the Lord hath laid on him the iniquity of us all." (Isaiah 53:6)

My mama told me that I'm depressed. She said that was the reason why I stay in bed on weekends and cry for hours and hours. Sometimes I stayed in my room with the lights off and curtains closed. A guidance counselor recommended that I get Prozac to get me through this, but Daddy says I only need to trust in the Lord. And pray. Often, I feel so empty in my heart and soul that I think my existence is shut off from the world. I have no energy. I have no fun. I feel hopeless and worthless.

"But let man and beast be covered with sackcloth and cry mightily unto God. Yea, let them turn everyone from his evil way and from the violence that is in their hands. Who can tell God if God will turn and repent and turn away from his fierce anger that we perish not?" (Jonah 3:8-9)

Daddy says women had seventy-four abortions last year for every 100 babies born in the city last year. This was double the national average. This is a godless place. A girl doesn't have too much time to wait before having an abortion. A girl doesn't have to notify her parents. It is too easy to terminate a life. It's open season to kill a fetus.

That is a terrible knowledge. These babies are being killed and thrown out with the trash. Once, in the bathroom, scrubbing the acne on my cheeks—red, angry blemishes—I screamed and screamed as I thought about this slaughter. The skin on my arms and legs started to shred, going down to the bones until the bone and flesh were exposed. Raw and painful.

Now, I look at my chewed-up fingernails. Suddenly, it all seems like a joke. I burst out laughing, laughing, laughing until I can't catch my breath.

"But I say unto you that every idle word that men shall speak, they shall give account thereof in the day of judgment." (Matthew 12:36)

Lettie, one of my girlfriends at school, had an older guy as a lover. She loved him totally. He left her just three weeks before they were to get married. She was crushed. We had been friends for more than eight years. Our parents had been friends. She came over that first night after he left, devastated and in tears. She had been faithful to him despite all the rumors that he had been playing around. She cried like a little girl. I held her head and let her tears wet my blouse. He was a great-looking guy but not really the kind I would have slept with. Then, she told me she was four months pregnant and was thinking about getting rid of it.

"He that believeth in the Son hath everlasting life, and he that believeth not in the Son shall not see life, but the wrath of God abideth on him." (John 3:36)

Daddy rebuked Lettie and her parents after he found out she was pregnant. Knocked up, as he called it. One night, I was listening when my parents went to bed, and they were talking in low tones, whispering. Mama told him something he hadn't known before. She said she was pregnant before they got together. A doctor friend of hers told her about a night nurse who did abortions. Mama had been pretty far along, so she went to the nurse who charged her $300 for the procedure. She said she felt funny that the abortion was done on the nurse's bed with a tarnished speculum. A boiled catheter was pushed through her cervix and left there. Mama almost died. She hid out at a girlfriend's house and suffered through three days of high fever, plenty of bleeding, chills, and she passed large gobs of tissue into the toilet. Her girlfriend's mother finally took her to the hospital where a doctor said her uterus was badly torn and infected. She was given a big dose of antibiotics and made to do bed rest. The hospital gave her a D&C and said she would probably not be able to have any more kids. But then she had me. As I'd kneeled beside their bedroom door, I heard a loud, resounding slap. And then a thud. My daddy's menacing voice made me shiver. "Damn it, Carole, why in the hell did you have to tell me that?" he'd shouted. From that night on, he treated her differently, as if she was a ghost in her own house.

"Let not sin therefore reign in your mortal body, that ye should obey it in the lusts thereof." (Romans 6:12)

I was wet behind the ears when I met Lettie. She took me to parties, get-togethers where my folks would have heart attacks if they'd known I was in those places. Plenty of street drama. Lots of girls competing to see if they could get some guy. It didn't matter how or why. Some of them yanked their tops down to show their tits or flashed their skirts up to show they were not wearing panties. They just wanted to have sex. I understood these women, but I wasn't as desperate as they were. Everything said, "I need a man." But what I knew a man was not going to solve their problems. In fact, a man could become a burden overnight. Still, these women sized up every man they went out with or bedded down to see if he could be a prospective husband. It was a weenie party supreme!

Motherhood was too complex and troubling. Getting pregnant was not difficult. Having a baby out of wedlock only made a bad situation worse. Lettie told me when she got drunk that all any girl wanted was someone to love and a guy who thought she was pretty. According to New York State law, Lettie's fetus was not a person when she aborted it.

"If we confess our sins, he is faithful and just to forgive our sins and to cleanse us from all unrighteousness." (1 John 1:9)

We drove in her Plymouth with her aunt to the abortion clinic in Riverdale to keep her appointment. There was a small crowd in front of the clinic, yelling slogans and holding placards and signs with bits of the Gospel or pictures of infants. Child murderers, they shouted. Some of these people I knew from past Operation Salvation campaigns. Others were recruits or kids. The cops who watched from cars would arrest them for trespassing, and they would be convicted and fined. Often, the leaders yelled that the rescue of a minor from the killers would mean one more young life. And God loves life.

I sat in the hallway with some of the parents and their girls. Most of them wore dour, plain clothes. I wanted to be with my friend. I followed, but one of the secretaries showed me out. I was angry. I wanted to see what they did to her. Maybe it was what they'd done to my mother. A fat, balding white man with a stethoscope dangling about his scrawny neck walked in and shook Lettie. I memorized his face. He said Lettie was in good hands and that he was a veteran of the abortion-rights movement. He was a child killer. The devil. He, and others like him, were the reason families were being destroyed.

After Lettie's abortion, I ride the train up there to Riverdale. I am no anti-abortion zealot. I am not a crazy who goes out to kill people. I snuck out of the house with the serious faces. Others pace and look out the windows at the protesters. I say the Lord's Prayer before I see the doctor drive up in his car. The same doctor who killed Lettie's baby.

I wished him dead. When I walked downtown, I often heard voices and was followed by people who change their faces and bodies at will. I haven't been able to sleep most nights. Three black cats crossed my path during the last week. My Aunt Alexis believed if a black cat sat on the bed of a sick person, the ill person would die. She really believed that dumb superstition. I dream of that same cat sauntering into the middle of my living room, and it talks, saying it can read my mind. When I try to head off the cat's words, it purrs and tells me before I can say something to stop it. And so, the black cat killed my aunt's friend, Maggie. She named the death of Maggie as a fact of that notion. Her heart attacks had come one after another, the anger and the blues rising inside her, and she died quickly. The pump just quit. Once, my Aunt Alexis laid eyes on me. She was a tortured soul who tried to deal with my demons by escaping into that crazy fantasy inside my head.

It takes a while. But I am patient. I see the devil doctor and know if I didn't do something to him, then my soul would be lost in the fires of eternal damnation. He is Satan himself. If something wasn't done to him, the poisonous reach of his evil would settle all over the county, all over the state, all over the world. I couldn't let him harm the innocents.

Now, here, the doctor walks past me and smiles, I nod and grin before I reach into my purse for the snub-nosed .38-caliber revolver. I touch him on the shoulder and let him turn to me.

"You are a baby killer," I say. Then, I shoot him in the face. "God loves life."

I shoot him three more times. Once in the neck, once in the chest, and another in the groin. I don't know why I did that.

But that was not how it happened. That was only how I imagined it. I think. Things are blurry now. That black cat cursing my mind.

I followed him home using my best friend, Peggy's car. I stalked him, jotting down the address of his home. I had an asthma attack, but it passed. I followed him and stood out on the lawn watching him.

I looked straight at the doctor through the window and reminded myself that he killed babies, tiny infants, and tiny souls. I'm sorry he kills life. A second after that the bullet pierced the top of his head, spraying red and gray matter on the walls of his house. His wife ran to him, almost catching his body in her arms. Her hand went to her open mouth, but the shrieks didn't come until later. She sank down to the floor, out of view. I heard her screams through the open window.

Later, I watch as the doctor's wife tells the TV reporter, her sad words choked with grief, about the murder.

"The wound to his head was scary," the wife says quietly. "I knew nobody could live with a wound like that. When I held him, he was still alive. He bled all over the place. His eyes were wide open, wide and frightened, just staring at the ceiling. His breaths got more labored, and then he stopped breathing."

The TV reporter puts the mike closer to the face of the wife to catch more detail, wanting to please the viewing public for the sake of the woman who laid with the devil doctor night after night. She wanted the wife to cry or show sorrow. Of course she did. TV people care about things like that.

Her red, puffy eyes stared at the reporter. "When that person pulled that trigger, he robbed us of a loving husband, a doting father, a compassionate doctor, and a generous man to his community. Damn you!"

A bad feeling goes through me, just like when you think somebody is watching you shower. I can't get her face out of my mind. I keep checking and rechecking my watch, washing and rewashing my hands, but I am never able to get them clean. They are red, raw and tender to the touch. I keep the forks and spoons all lined up the same way in the tray. I do this again and again, watching from the kitchen.

The other picture they show is the doctor's clinic, decorated with banks and banks of flowers, teddy bears, cards, and other tributes from his admirers. His stupid fans. Five cops guard the front of the building which the reporter says has been vandalized and firebombed. Good.

"He," the wife had said, was her husband's killer. She never said the word she. I thought I got away with the murder.

Later, when my legs gave out, and I collapsed, Daddy caught

me in his powerful arms, caught me against his cotton shirt and held my body tightly. I cried. I remember that.

"I've done a wrong thing, Daddy," I whispered into his ear. "But I avenged a great sin. I killed the baby-killer."

Daddy must have called the cops. I was sitting down in a chair on the back porch. People screamed and cried. I borrowed a cigarette from somebody. It was the first cigarette I'd ever had.

A detective on the TV had said the doctor should have worn a bullet-proof vest to prevent something like this.

When the cops came, I identified myself and told them I was the proud daughter of a Christian minister. I told them I killed the doctor for God, but I did it for my mama, my aunt, my grandma, and all the women in the country too.

Blasphemy

This was the third birthday their mother had sent for me. It seemed as though nobody else would do. She told me once that she tried other escort services, but they did not satisfy. Her boys, the Siamese twins conjoined at the head, meant something special to her. Nothing but the best would do for them.

She found me in an ad touting my skills some time ago. Yes, this was the third birthday in a row. I knew a lot about her. When her husband left her about fourteen years ago, she went back to night school and became a lawyer. There were stories in the newspapers after he left her, made her famous or at least notorious. Society does not like ambitious, independent, smart women. They didn't like that she didn't seem to need a man even though she had special needs.

On the other hand, I got out of school and took my GED. The want ads did not do anything for me. I pounded the pavement but no luck. My parents didn't want me to stay there, said they had three other kids to raise, and I was setting a bad example. To be truthful, I was not into boys. Maybe I tongue-kissed Howard and let Dave feel my breasts, but that was it. My Uncle Linus swatting me on the behind a couple of times was the extent of my sex life for a long time.

Then there was Maurice. He was my first. He was crude, vulgar, and forceful. We went on a date, saw one of the *Candyman* movies, where you say his name three times, and he appears. Candyman, Candyman. You get my drift. Maurice finger-fucked me in the show, made me smell his finger, and then demanded I sit on him. Hurt like hell. I bled, and we started screwing every chance we got. He was forty-six. I was sixteen.

My parents cautioned me against older men. But I liked them. They knew more than the guys my age who couldn't teach me shit. Owen was responsible for turning me out. He went down on me. I went down on him. His favorite position was doggie-style, or up against the refrigerator, or nibbling my ear. That really set me off. Owen was thirty-six.

"Take off your clothes, close your eyes and turn around," Owen said, holding a Magic Wand vibrator between my thighs.

"Will it hurt?" I asked, feigning shyness. I knew it wouldn't.

"No. Just let me do a little circular motion," he said, massaging my sex.

I couldn't catch my breath. It was the first time I really came. A short time after that, we moved into a flat on the Upper West Side together. I was in love.

It seemed like nothing, the first time. I'd sat in a BMW beside Owen who tried to get his friend Kevin to have sex with me. Owen said he had to pay his car note. If I really loved him, I would do this, he said. Kevin was his boy, so it would not be like I was cheating or something, he said. Kevin kept saying I had a nice ass. I did it so Owen could pay his bill.

Then, an older guy from his job lost his wife. Felix talked to Kevin who talked to Owen about the old man needing an emotional lift. Owen was against it at first. He was afraid I could fall for him because I had a thing about father figures. That Freud shit. I didn't want to do it. Owen slapped me and called me a bitch. Money changed hands, and I went with the sad old guy. I didn't screw him. I don't think he could have stood a real fucking. But I went down on him. I rinsed my mouth out with Listerine after. Owen hated the taste of spunk.

"You taking the pill or the IUD?" Owen asked me one day.

"The pill," I said confidently. I heard the IUD can scar up your pussy.

"So how many weeks are you late?" he quizzed me.

"I don't know," I replied. I was over two months late.

"Do you know whose it is?"

"No. You made sure of that." My wisecrack earned me a slap.

A few days later, he got me an abortion from some doctor. Clean, safe, and efficient. I was out there taking clients again in two weeks. Owen said he had bills to pay.

Justine was another one of his girls. She was always trying to make the moves on me. I caught her smelling my panties once. That was gross. Owen had nine girls two years ago. Justine got obsessed with this Cuban girl. She was totally crazy about her. Owen knew there was going to be trouble. He caught them doing each other, but he couldn't keep them apart. Finally, Justine split with the Cuban girl, stole some money, and a car. Owen reported it to the police, and the car was discovered in Kansas City. No sign of the girls.

Dakota, a girl mixed with Native American and Cajun blood, entered my life and completely changed how I saw womanhood. She talked to me about the art of orgasms, Tantric sex, pleasuring a clit, and the roles of tops and bottoms. I couldn't get enough of her. She became my sister and confidante.

"Are you kinky, Marie?" she once asked me.

"I think so," I answered, figuring I'd probably done everything in the book sexually, especially some of the kinkier stuff.

"How you been with a woman?" she asked, her eyebrows raised.

"Sure. Many times." Some of my more joyous experiences had been with women, who offered gentler, more tender sexual exchanges.

"Threesomes or foursomes?"

"Yes. Owen arranged those for me," I replied. "They were fun."

"You like gay men?"

"Sure. Did you know Owen is bi?" I asked.

"I know that," she said matter-of-factly. "Do you have a short black dress?"

"Yes."

She took over my life. "Wear it and meet me at this address in Tribeca."

It was the address of Fletcher, a redhead dyke, who worked as a criminal court judge in her spare time. Her loft was sheer artistry. Modern yet tasteful, something straight out of *House Beautiful*. The place was crowded with older guys, college girls who figured they could take a walk on the wild side before graduation, middle-aged lesbians willing to seduce frigid women dissatisfied with married life, oddball neo-sexuals, coke-crazy stock traders, and a herd of hookers who just liked to have a good time.

Fletcher introduced me to the wife of a minor UN diplomat, a worldly woman who knew the ropes and ushered me into a private rear room. The wife's husband, a Greek, sat beside the bed as we ran through our carnal appetites, panting like sheepdogs until he joined us. I let him fuck me while she sat on my face. We switched places. He lasted for hours, well after Dakota left for her apartment. They invited me back to their place in Gramercy Park, but I declined. I was totally bushed.

"Did you have fun, Marie?" Dakota asked, when she saw me that weekend.

I grinned and covered my sex with my hands, sore and bruised but loving it.

She winked and pointed at me with her finger like the spotlight was on me. Maybe it was. Maybe not.

I thought back to my world clocks ago. The past. Man, the world once revolved around me, Marie Larson, or so my folks thought. That was how they expected my life to go. This pretty young woman was to be treated like royalty wherever I went. According to Uncle Isaac, I was so beautiful that just looking at me hurt your eyes. Something happens to a girl when the people she knows fall silent when they are in her presence when the women start clucking their tongues at how developed she was for a tall, comely teenager just past the bud of adolescence. But they turned on me. Everybody turned on me. I was the enemy. I was the alien because of my beauty. And beauty translates into sexiness. So, I had to be a whore. I guess it was preordained, divined, a prophesy foretold.

"Marie, you be careful out there with those men." Mama Larson counseled me when she saw something unspeakable come into her man's eyes after I walked across the kitchen completely topless.

My father was in the doghouse for two months after pulling that stunt. Looking at his own flesh-and-blood like she was a common hussy in the street. Mama Larson was having none of that kind of foolishness under her roof. Too much of that sinful lust occurred in these parts, fathers who forgot their place and touched their daughters in a manner that ought to be reserved for their womenfolk.

Once, Mama stood in the doorway my bedroom, watching me prance and rock back and forth while I applied rouge to my pouty lips. Feeling sexy, I hunched over the dresser facing the mirror, enjoying the power of my splendid youth. My mother shook her head as if her mind wrestled with the sinister notion of some man's calloused, rough hands pawing at the soft, tender skin of this girl who marveled at how men seemed eager to grant her every wish.

"Marie, I don't want you hanging down at the pizza shop so much," her father said. His harsh expression chilled my very soul. "You are getting much too big to be running around these streets like you don't have a care in the world. At sixteen, you must carry yourself like a young lady, so everyone knows you deserve respect. Do you know what I'm telling you?"

"I think so," I said, in that thumb-sucking, coy voice that drove him nuts. "I don't do nothing. I just mind my own business."

My father knew better. The reports were coming daily, full of Marie sightings, my lithe body crammed in too tight blouses and cut-off jeans, and that walk that whispered of things that only grown-ups dared to do behind closed doors. Lewd, evil, depraved things he said he could not even imagine as a good Christian man. Now, he tried to keep a close eye on me, on what I wore, where I went, what I did.

"We have a name to maintain, girlie," my father snarled, spinning me around so he could gauge the hemline height of the bright-blue summer dress I wore that day. "You can't wear this out in the street. If you bend over to pick something up, people can see all your rear end. You oughta be ashamed of yourself."

I frowned and stood with my hands on my hips. "I don't see anything wrong with what I got on. All the girls wear their dresses this short. It's the fad. Even the movie stars wear them this short."

"Honey, come and look at what your daughter has got on," my father shouted. "It's an abomination."

"Oh no, you don't!" my mother shrieked, when she entered the room. "Take that off right now. You're not going out of this house looking like that. You've got to be kidding, take that off now!"

When my mother put her foot down, there was no debate, no back-talk, no hemming and hewing. She took a stand, and that was that. Her word was law. Even my father knew better than to question her mandates, her declarations, for the consequences could be hellish. She was serious, very serious.

I stormed past her, pouting and mumbling under my breath. "You never let me do nothing. You watch me like a hawk. You don't trust me. You treat me like a child."

"What did you say?" My mother moved quickly behind me like an angry schoolmarm. "Speak up and let me hear you. Don't say something that'll get you in hot water."

I slowed to a mincing walk, intentionally wiggling my bottom like a street whore until I got to the bathroom and slammed the door. There I stayed for hours, sitting on the toilet, plotting my escape from the iron tyranny of my parents. I would wait until they went to bed, were sound asleep, and then I would walk quietly to the door, like a stalking cat, open it and slip away into the darkness.

But the police brought me back. Brought me back three times. Until my parents kicked me out.

Dakota thinks I'm a submissive. Sexually submissive. She says I provoke Owen so he can give me black eyes and busted lips. I don't know about that. I love strong men. I hate wimps and sensitive guys who cry on cue. They might as well be faggots. When Dakota said it, I never thought about it. Submissive? Maybe.

I had a lot of partners. I love sex. But Mario was special. He could be so nice, smiling one minute and whipping your ass, literally, the next. He always gave me a safe word in case he went too far. Mario loved to dominate women. When I first met him at a party, I walked in on him, and he had a woman blindfolded with a ball gag in her mouth. Her breasts were bound tightly, and her wrists and legs were secured too. I pulled up a seat and watched him and his dark art.

Mario's first words to me: "Light me a cigarette." The delivery was Bogie-style. Humphrey Bogart, gangster, all the way.

He winked at me, tightened the ropes, and squatted down to put his dick into her mouth. She sucked like an infant at a teat. I almost came. No shit.

I waited for the woman outside, chatted her up, and went for a coffee with her.

Fueled by caffeine, she rattled on and on about pain and pleasure. The people in the art form were brilliant, attune to the senses of the body, she said.

I asked her about Mario.

She raved about his magic, the holy merging of the dual sensations, and his capable alchemy in matters of the flesh.

At the time, I had a wonderful relationship with Donnie, a car salesman. He cared for me in every way. He listened to me when I talked, and if I needed something, he got it for me. He was very gentle and very attentive. But I was restless sexually. He was all right, but I wanted more. I started having sex with strangers, bruisers, novices who thought they knew what I wanted. I wanted to be tortured and humiliated. Donnie could never turn me on, not in a million years.

Mario allowed me to fantasize, violent, cruel fantasies. The first session, he tied up my breasts and flogged them. He followed that up with blindfold games. On the second occasion, he spanked me, licked me, and whipped me across the back lightly with a leather strap. The third time, he tied me up and raped me.

Donnie noticed the bruises that night and yelled at me. He cleaned them, washed them out with peroxide, and dressed the major cuts.

I told Mario I was in a committed relationship—a no-no—and he flipped the hell out. I needed him to slap me around. I know it's twisted.

I broke up with Donnie to be with Mario, but he wouldn't forgive me. He wouldn't return my calls. I finally gave up.

Submissive? Dakota was right. She read my thoughts, I think.

It was their birthday, the boys I told you about before. They were in their late teens. Their mother wheeled out a cake with a forest fire of burning candles, marble icing, and strawberries inside. The boys, with their heads attached at the crown, lay on an adjustable table. She had dressed them nicely—a gray leisure suit on one and a dark blue suit on the other. They were immaculately groomed.

"How old are they now?" I asked, wondering what I would do for them.

The woman didn't answer me. She was too busy gathering their gifts, piling them on the sofa in a pyramid. Stacks of ribboned boxes upon boxes. Balloons, all colors, were stuck on the ceiling.

"They're eighteen. They're men now." Their mother smiled.

She pulled me to the kitchen, sat at the table, and poured me a drink. Vodka. She had one too. Her face winced as it went down.

"You've got a nice home here," I said, looking around.

"It's better than the old one." She laughed. "Remember up in the Bronx? I hated the way the neighbors used to look at them. Like they were freaks. That would tear me up inside."

"I've always wanted to ask you a question." I drank my drink.

"What is that, darling?" She lit a cigarette.

"How did you get them out of you?"

"Caesarian section. There was no way they could have gotten them out otherwise." She laughed. "They cut them out."

"Was it hard? I'm so afraid of childbirth." I couldn't imagine a pregnancy like hers.

"Yes, their father left me without any money or anything," she said, her anger fresh enough for me to hear it. "I should have had them separated. The doctors said I couldn't have done that at birth. I was scared. You know, the surgery isn't like it is these days. If I had told them yes, it would have probably been death for them."

"I've always wondered how they would do it. Cut their heads?" I felt totally dumb as soon as I said it. *Dumb-ass.*

"I don't know," she replied. "The doctors said it would take hours to separate them at the top of their heads. I think he said twenty hours. Then, after that, they would still have to give them additional surgery, for complications like infection or swelling in their brains. It was a long, drawn-out process."

"But they seem normal in every way," I said cheerily.

"Yes, they do." She seemed off in her mind far away as if she was thinking about what it would be like to have been a woman with a normal, healthy childbirth. Had kids that weren't freaks. Everybody stopping and looking at them. She waved me into their bedroom, with my little gifts for both and the best present, me. I was going to rock their world.

Still, I had to get used to them again—the twins joined at the enormous head, the little dwarf bodies, tiny hands and feet, skinny legs, but not so small organs. It seemed the Lord made up for their odd proportions when he put those things on them. They were the size of an infant's fat arm, brown and wrinkly with huge veins on them. The boys loved me to service them with my mouth. They'd giggle, their tongues hanging out, their eyes rolling back in their heads.

I always wondered if the boys felt the same sensations when I worked on one and not the other. They seemed to smile, but you never knew. This is the strangest job I've had.

The twins were sprawled on a king-sized bed. They watched me walk into the room, put my bag down and pull up a chair. I noticed first thing the posters of the female movie stars and singers—Nia Long, Charlize Theron, Halle Berry, Whitney Houston, Meg Ryan, Jennifer Lopez, Paris Hilton, Pamela Anderson—plastered all around the room. I smiled, thinking the twins were just like any guy—sex, sex, and more sex.

"Gavin had Mom put them up," George, the more subdued twin, said. He smiled. "Do you like them?"

"What's not to like?" I said. "Hey, if I were a dyke, I'd get with Halle Berry myself." That cracked them up.

"We thought you wouldn't come," Gavin said. "You said you'd call regularly after you visited the last time. It gets lonely locked away in this room."

I felt bad. "You know I'm busy all the time. That doesn't mean I don't think about you. I always think of you."

George pouted. "But you didn't call."

"That's not true," I said. "I called several times, but your mother said you were asleep."

Both said in a low voice, "She is a lying bitch." It always spooked me out when they said the same thing at the same time.

"She doesn't want us to have any friends," Gavin said. "There used to be a girl who visited us from down the hall. About sixteen. She was nice. We would sit and talk about teenager stuff. Mom chased her away."

George's eyes narrowed. "She always chases them away. The girl was nice. Like you."

"Want a cigarette?" I offered them one as I took a cancer stick from my purse.

They didn't say anything, just watched me light it and inhale the smoke.

"I'd like to get a few puffs on it," Gavin, the more rambunctious of the pair, said. "Hey, I'm eighteen. I am a man now."

George didn't like the idea of the smoke going into his body, their body. "I hate cigarette smoke. It makes me cough. Mom smokes. The apartment is full of smoke. I wish I could have fresh air. The nanny, this West Indian woman, used to take us out to the park. Boy, I liked that. Fresh air, kids laughing, guys running past on their jogs."

"Well, I want to get a puff or two," Gavin said. "Just put it up to my lips."

I looked at George, who nodded his approval. He loved his brother. They relied on each other for everything. I put it up to Gavin's lips, and he inhaled it and blew it out of his nose.

George coughed like the smoke was stuck in his throat. "Just joking." He laughed.

"You know what my birthday wish is?" Gavin asked.

"What?" I gulped down some smoke and put it out.

"I want Mom dead," he said. "We've talked about it. She had a chance to separate us, but she didn't. She treats us like freaks. We can't have any company. She is so mean to us, yells and curses at us. She thinks she could have lived a normal life if she didn't have us."

I sat down on the chair, frowning. "She is sad. Maybe depressed. She thinks her life would have been different, but she loves you. Loves both of you guys."

"Bullshit," both boys said.

"Why do you say that?" I asked. "She does everything for you. She sacrifices for you, and you don't want for anything. I think you are ungrateful. That's what I think."

Gavin spoke slowly and menacingly. "Do you know what she does? She charges people to see us. Sometimes, the apartment is packed with people who just stand and stare and ask stupid questions. She has a large Chinese puzzle box full of money. And every week, she goes to the bank and deposits it."

"We're tired of being treated like trained seals," George said. "Like freaks."

"And she has a group of mothers who have children who are freaks—two heads, six arms, three legs. You get my meanings," Gavin said angrily. "It's nationwide. They have fundraisers and benefits. And she goes around, giving talks. It's a racket, and we're tired of being exploited."

"Do you understand what we're talking about?" George asked. "How far did you go in school?"

I fidgeted with my thumbs. "I dropped out."

"Hmm, but do you know what we're talking about?" George asked. "Do you get me?"

"Yes, I do." I hated when people tried to act like I'm stupid because I didn't finish school. I'm not a dummy. And these guys, well, my life was better than theirs. That was for sure.

Gavin asked if I put the cigarette out. I said yeah. He asked me if I could light another one. I felt these boys had been planning this for a long time—a plot to rid the world of Mom, and maybe get their freedom. Or something.

"Do people think you are living a decent life?" George asked. "They probably think you are as much of a freak as we are. They don't think you're normal. They don't think you should be selling yourself. It's not moral, right?"

"Hey, I'm not the brightest bulb in the circuit, but I get by," I said. "So, what are you trying to say?" I was getting mad.

"Nothing," the boys said in unison.

"So, tell me more about why you want to get rid of your mother."

Gavin placed the cigarette to his mouth with his short fingers. "You want to know more? One thing is the male company she keeps. They're bastards. Jerks all. One drunk asshole stood right over my bed and pissed on us. Another put out cigarettes on us."

"We're tired of being abused," George insisted. "She has got to go."

"I hate the bitch," Gavin said. "She'll give us castor oil and let us mess on ourselves, and then we have to lay in here smelling our own shit. It's disgusting."

"That is her punishment if we don't do right," George said. They watched me like they wanted to see my response.

I was shocked by everything they told me.

"Kill her, kill her, kill her," they said. The effect was like an eerie choir.

"And what do I get for all my trouble?" I asked.

Just then, their mother knocked on the door and popped her head into the room. "Hey Marie, you're not even undressed. I want you to give them their fun, and then we can cut the cake and open the presents. Chop, chop, Marie. Hurry, okay?"

"I will." I laughed and took off my red silk blouse.

As soon as the door closed, the boys went on detailing their terrifying plan from start to finish. They said I would get the money in the Chinese box, the small safe behind the painting of Sidney Poitier, and some trinkets in a safety deposit box at the bus station. All I had to do was kill her. Cut her throat and let the life flow out of her.

"How will you live?" I asked. "There will be nobody to take care of you."

Gavin and George had thought it all out. I would return that evening, dressed in black with a veil. I would kneel in front of their publicity photograph, say something from a holy scroll and then pour palm wine over their picture. I would gently place the boys in the tub, give them a drink from the wine and give them a moment to reflect on what their lives would have been if they were normal guys. Then I would pour the gasoline all over them and strike the match.

"What do you think of our plan?" George asked.

I couldn't answer. I was stunned. This was the last thing I wanted to get into today. I wanted to fuck, collect my money, and say goodbye. Now, this intrigue and shit. I cried. I cry at the drop of a hat. My heart gets easily crushed. Their story touched me. I don't know why, but it did. When they said they were freaks, and so was I, that was the truth. I have never felt at ease in this world. I always felt like an outsider, like an irregular weave. A misfit.

"I don't know," I replied.

"The money is there if you want it," Gavin said. "What can you lose?"

I folded my arms and sat back. "I can get caught."

"There's enough money for you to live on for a while," George said. "If you live within your means, you could live really good. Think about it."

"Aren't you tired of your life?" Gavin added.

"Yes, I am." I was honest. I wanted out. I wanted to live life like normal people. No more whoring.

"Kill her, and your life can change," the boys said in tandem. "If you think about it, you won't do it. Just do it. Think about it afterward as you count the money."

There was a lecherous glint in Gavin's eyes as his fingers tried to lower his trousers. "Here, can you undo this?" he asked, after he looked at George who shook his head.

What a time to think about sex. I leaned over the bed, undid his zipper, and placed him in my mouth.

After I finished servicing the boys, I went to find their mother, who was washing the dishes. She had a cup of coffee at her elbow. Plates, wet and shiny, were filed in a rack. Four pots and a cast-iron skillet sat turned face-down on the sink. Her back was to me, her hands gripping a grease and suds covered pie pan.

"Did you give the boys your present?" she asked, when I came into the room.

"Yeah, I gave it to them," I said coolly.

She turned her face slightly to the left and kept scrubbing the pie pan. "What's wrong with you? You don't sound happy."

I reached for a butcher knife from among the knives on the kitchen table, a wooden handled slicer, and I put it behind my back. Three little steps carried me to her while she kept chattering away about nothing.

"What mother would give her boys a wonderful gift like you?" She laughed as if she felt smug about her charity.

I laughed nervously.

She spun around and saw the knife and pushed out her hands in a defensive fashion, to keep me from harming her face. Her face registered shock, wonder, and surprise.

I plunged the knife into her chest.

Her hands went to the wound, and she fell into the table.

I kept stabbing her arms, side, stomach, cheek, and shoulder.

She screamed once. Just once.

To my surprise, she punched me in the face, temporarily stunning me, and causing me to drop the knife. Then, she fell, as if her legs wouldn't hold her up. She crawled on the kitchen floor, leaving a trail of blood on the black-and-white tiles.

I pounced on her, stabbing the blade into her back over and over.

She gave a hoarse rattle into the floor, a gurgling, and then lay still.

I put my ear to her back and listened. She was dead.

For several minutes, I crouched near her face, listening for signs of life. I stood up, wiped my damp forehead, and staggered to the sink. My reflex was to throw the knife into the soapy water. Instead, I washed the knife, carefully and slowly, from handle to blade. I didn't touch the body.

I stepped over it, not touching anything. Weary, I walked down the hallway toward the boys' bedroom. I opened the door, emotionally drained, but I was happy to keep up my part of the bargain.

"The police are on their way. Should be here in a few minutes," Gavin said. He gave a dry, bitter laugh. He had a small silver pistol in his hand. "You've played your part in this little drama. And now it's our turn."

I was surprised. Suddenly, I realized I'd been conned like the fool I was. "You gotta to be damn kidding."

Both boys said in soul harmony like background singers, "No, we aren't."

I sat in the chair by their bed and put my head down because the room was spinning. *I am a fool. I am a fool. I am a stupid-ass fool. I am a fool.*

The boys must have seen it all on my face. I'd trusted them. I thought they, like the boys who had sampled my body before them, were truthful and just misunderstood. That was my problem; I believed everyone. I was one dumb bitch. Even when it meant a royal fuck-up like this one.

"Do you have any more of those cigarettes?" Gavin asked, keeping the gun pointed at my head. "Could you light one for me, please? The police will be here shortly."

Summer Comes Later

Looking out the car window, he saw the red oasis city of Marrakesh in the distance, toward the dark outline of the mountains. Ahead, three men in ragged djellabas herded a flock of sheep along the road. The truck in front of him weaved wildly back and forth, then jerked to a sudden stop before the sea of unruly wool. The abrupt halt of his ancient Saab sent the entire backseat cargo sailing through the humid air, down into a jumble on the floor—his camera equipment, thermos, a pair of battered suitcases, and crumpled bags of figs and dates.

He recognized that he was in exile, away from New York. Fleeing from America. Historically, he was not the first writer in his late thirties to seek a place of solace other than home, the troubled land of his birth, to recover and heal. Baldwin did it. Hemingway did it. Many of his countrymen did it. Still, none of his pals understood why he would walk away from a good-paying job on a newspaper to catch his breath.

He was a refugee of the wounded heart and tarnished romance. He'd had his moment of glory, his day in the sun, his fifteen minutes of fame, and then it had been all downhill. Like so many baby boomers, he felt the aggression of the hungry, skilled young reporters, half his age, who were not scarred by the memories of Jim Crow, determined to make their mark in the business. He saw them ruthlessly pushing forward throughout the industry, breaking through on every level, more comfortable with whites and the corporate world than he ever could be.

This was what he was up against. This was what his wife never understood. In her mind, he had never achieved his potential and had failed their dream.

His moment under the media sun's glistening rays had come when he'd interviewed Yasir Arafat in the early 1980s in a small pock-marked building in Beirut, Lebanon. A car, full of the man's private staff, all armed, had picked him up at his hotel and driven him blindfolded into the Arab quarter. He'd been guided, staggering, into a room, where the blinders were removed. A short, bearded man sat before him at a long table with a large Palestinian flag mounted on the wall behind him. The first thing he'd noticed about Arafat was his drab-green military fatigues and the large holstered gun on his hip.

"It is the will of Allah that I lead my people back to their homeland, that I overcome the Jewish invaders," Arafat had said, staring at him as if he were an alien being. "This struggle will not be won overnight. It will take years, maybe generations, to come, but it will come. Before it is over, there will be much war waged in the name of peace. Many will die, but peace will come."

When he'd tried to question the PLO leader about the so-called Islamic menace to peace, Muslim extremists, the wild card of Arabian oil, and the interference of the West in the battle for a homeland, Arafat reminded him of the sacking of the Holy Temple of Jerusalem by the Romans in A.D. 70. The calling for a Jewish state of Palestine by Theodor Herzl in 1887, the dominance of the British during the late 1930s, the 1947

Partition. The first war by the Arabs against the Jews shortly after that and the annexing of the West Bank by Jordan and the Gaza by Egypt.

Without a doubt, it was a history lesson rendered slowly and expertly by the tiny man with the penetrating dark eyes. "You must know how we feel to be forced from one place to another, nomads, never at home anywhere," Arafat said, through clenched teeth. "Your people endured it as slaves, so it must not be a strange feeling for you to understand."

Every foreign reporter he knew had warned him how shrewd and perceptive Arafat could be, possessing skills that often misled journalists into underestimating him, much to their chagrin. But he would not be fooled. He researched the leader, reading of his early days as a founder of the Al Fatah, the guerrilla army formed to fight the Israelis in 1959, to his post in the fledgling PLO in the mid-1960s, to his ascension to PLO chairman in 1969. When the PLO was kicked out of Jordan in 1970, Arafat and the boys moved to Beirut.

"Why aren't you writing this down?" Arafat asked. He motioned to one of his aides.

"Well, this is pretty much background," the writer replied, holding his pad up. "I'm waiting for your response to my questions about any movement to the peace process."

Arafat picked up the telephone and spoke quietly into it. While the leader talked, one of his men tried to place his chief in context, speaking softly about his exploits in battle, the speeches, and the botched assassination attempts. Arafat was indeed a survivor.

"Someone must pay the cost of peace, take it on, and not be afraid to die," Arafat continued, after the phone call ended. "I'm not popular with anyone. The guns are pointed at my head from every direction. Let me ask you this. Do you think the Americans will ever accept us as they do the Jews?"

The two men talked for almost three hours nonstop, and the result was a series of articles—*Arafat Speaks!*—that brought him praise and book offers back in the West. That was then. That was before the days of the great drought.

Now, he was back in the region, following up leads about fundamentalist hardliners, terrorist cells, threats to American embassies, and the changing winds of the Islamic Jihad. On the road to Marrakesh, he understood that his nerves were frayed at the edges, unraveling swiftly. Nothing could prevent him from doing something stupid.

Tempers flared in the white glare of the noonday sun. He watched the men in the truck descend on the Berber herders, arms waving, shouting in harsh Arabic for the herders to clear a path. Fierce and proud, the Berbers took their time, moving at a slow, regal pace, casually guiding the animals to the road's narrow shoulders with well-aimed pokes of their sticks. Behind him, others grew impatient, filling the air with sharp curses, guttural threats, and the angry barks of their car horns.

Sitting behind the steering wheel of his aging car, wrapped in the stifling Moroccan heat, his mind went back to his beloved ex-wife Janet, her satiny voice in his head mixing in seamless unison with the cacophony of the mayhem outside. The tape played on, spilling brine onto his internal wounds, triggering that bone-deep ache, the bitter regret of his failed marriage.

Finally, the traffic moved, winding up the road toward the city. Woozy from the long drive from Tangiers, he tried to remember his first trip to Morocco in the 1970s, when he stayed at the El Monsour in Casablanca, the Rebat Hilton, and the grand old Momounia in Marrakesh. He was a kid

145

then, in his early twenties. His father gave him the trip after reading Paul Bowles' novel *The Sheltering Sky* about Port and Kit trying to jump-start their dull lives with an ill-fated trip to the desert, the vast, merciless Sahara. His father, ever the academic with his literature class at Columbia, stood with him in the air terminal, going through his checklist of essentials for international travel.

First, travel light. Second, buy your medicines such as aspirin, cold medications, and toiletries before leaving the States. Third, and most important, keep your Traveler's Checks, credit cards, and cash on your person, in an inside jacket pocket and not in your carry-on luggage or other suitcases. Fourth, lock up your valuables in the hotel safe. Don't leave them unprotected in your hotel room. All good advice. Being well-traveled, the old man knew what he was talking about.

This time, in Marrakesh, he stayed in a small hotel not far from the city's Holiday Inn, which featured adequately sized rooms with telephone and old Philco televisions harking back to the glory days of Milton Berle and Sid Caesar. After checking in, he sat on the queen-sized bed, thinking of taking a stroll down near Hotel Layesh where there was always action and a questionable clientele. Kif peddlers. Quick-fingered thieves. Burned-out torch singers. Forsaken women on carnal display, outside of the protection of the Qur'an. Dangerous at night, it was also not particularly safe to stroll down there in daylight.

The telephone rang. It was Dr. Mrabet, a great friend of his father and his old Columbia professor of Middle Eastern literature and philosophy. Word was he possessed a connection to several terrorist groups in the region, some of them violent and extreme.

"William, welcome to Marrakesh," the doctor said. "So, what

are your plans?"

"Following up a story on the Al Kufir. They say the hardcore extremists have had their hands in many of the terrorist attacks in Israel, Egypt, Jordan, Yemen, Pakistan, India, and Afghanistan," he answered. "I'm waiting for a contact, someone to get me inside."

"Maybe that's a story you should leave alone," the doctor replied. "One you should step away from. Come around and see me. We'll talk about old times."

"Why do you say I should leave it alone?"

"Because there are some things you should not bother. Walk away and go home. These people are fundamentalists devoted to the Islamic Jihad. I don't think they're people you want to aggravate. You're an American. They hate Americans. I say leave it alone and go home."

"I can't," he said. "I've got to take a chance. I need this one."

The doctor switched gears. "Why aren't you married, a good-looking man like you?"

"Our marriage didn't take," I said. "My wife stopped loving me. I came here to get my head on straight. To heal. And to win a Pulitzer by doing the first inside story on Al Kufir. I can't leave until I do that."

"Do you know what I'm hearing, William?" The doctor's voice had a bite to it.

"What?"

"There is talk around the city that you're not just a journalist, that you are something else. A spy, a CIA operative. Believe me, if you go digging for your story in the wrong quarters, you will be killed. These are very serious, dedicated people. The streets are not safe. There have been shootings, bombings, kidnappings of foreigners, and other things. General unrest.

The police and army are everywhere. Be careful, please."

The spy comment struck a nerve. "So, that's what they say. Well, I am what I say I am."

The doctor laughed. "Tell that to the men who follow you. My son, your every move is being watched. If you stay here, you're a marked man. Enough about this story. We'll talk more when I see you."

"I look forward to that," he replied.

"*Insha'allah.* Worry not because Allah makes all things right," the doctor said. "He is merciful, compassionate, and fair. If you are meant to get this story, it will be so. Nothing can stop it from happening if it is the will of Allah. Worry not, my son. What is meant to be cannot be stopped."

The phone went silent. After the call, William reviewed his notes, checked the addresses from his sources, and fell asleep on the bed. It was just a matter of time.

At dusk, he remained holed up, awaiting word about whether the righteous would welcome him, an infidel, into their world. While he waited, he watched a nude couple in their room across the way through the window. He could see everything. The woman knew how to work her magic. Her Arab lover did his part as well, letting her straddle him on the bed as she kissed and licked the soft brown skin of his broad chest around his nipples. At times, she indulged in her love play as if her life depended on the heat of her passion. But there were moments when the fervent kisses, frenzied caresses, and demented wails bordered on fake, like something out of a well-rehearsed strip show, a practiced lie. She rode him hard and strong, the man's hairy hands worrying her moist sex underneath the cloth while her fingers encircled his neck. When his nature had been sufficiently aroused, and his sap was high, he applied his tongue to the tender skin near her navel and down to the curly cleft between her legs. Her screams of joy echoed in the air to mix with the occasional murmur of gunfire. Her Arab lover tilted the amber glow of the lamp as he moved to re-enter her so the watcher could see his thin, craggy face. Once the brown man plunged into her again, he never took his eyes off the stranger across the alley until she trembled violently once or twice underneath him, her sweaty legs locked tightly around his gleaming buttocks. The Arab man knew the dark American was watching them.

Watching them brought it all back. Janet and the days before the crack-up. He felt utterly alone now, cut off from the world, from all tenderness, love, or redemption. Despair, terror, and gloom landed against his chest like a series of cruel, vicious slaps.

"Sweetheart," Janet, his wife had said the night before she left him.

"What, baby?"

"William, tell me you'll never leave me. Tell me you love me." She was toying with him. The marriage was already dead.

He never answered her, mumbled something under his breath, and rolled away from her, angered that she'd even asked that of him.

When his editor called two hours later from New York, his eyes were swollen from crying. His voice was thick with tears and words stuck in his throat.

None of it was lost on the white man who had hired him when no one else would, especially for a big-time city daily. "How's the story coming?" his editor asked, his tone cheery.

"It's a waiting game, but I expect something to break any day now. I've put some feelers out, and the fish are circling. I expect a nibble soon."

"Bill, we believe in you. But we can't foot the bill for you to take a vacation. We expect results. Find the rag heads you need to talk to and get this thing over with. And don't take any unnecessary chances."

"Yeah, you bet," he said, then hung up. Outside, police sirens had sounded in an annoying chorus.

If it is the will of Allah. What is meant to be cannot be stopped. If it is the will of Allah. He looked out of the window toward the hotel across the street, hoping for a distraction from the room where the young Arab couple met every day. But the shade was down, and there was nothing to see. Not a damn thing to watch. Killing time, he sprawled on the bed, completely nude, smoking cigarette after cigarette. As the ashtray filled and the black telephone on the nightstand near his bed remained silent, he became more and more anxious. Then, his mind wandered back a few years to when he covered a rash of terrorist bombings in Tangiers committed by a new splinter-group determined to shake up the status quo.

Once, in Tangiers, he'd seen a woman, dressed in rather risque Western clothes, being shunned by other Arabs walking along one of the city's narrow side streets. Her head and eyebrows were shaved, much like the French woman collaborators of the Nazis, who were marched through cobbled Parisienne streets after the second world war. The unforgiving crowd parted for her, this vessel of condemned female flesh, like the stacked waters of the Red Sea under the power of Moses' blessed staff. As he'd neared the scarlet woman, he'd seen alarm and fear in her dark eyes and in the contorted expressions of the others as they went out of their way to move around her, avoiding all contact. His companion, Abu Omar, a writer from a local Arab newspaper, had cautioned him to steer clear of her as well. No talking or touching.

The woman's beauty was in her modern attitude, her courage to be bold, at least that was what he'd told himself. To her, he was just another American infidel. As she passed him, her gaze changed from fear to a sharp look of disdain, and she marched past with her head held arrogantly aloft. Each of her proud steps sounded a brutal note of contempt for both him and the crowd.

Eventually, the memories of the woman and Tangiers dis- solved into another fit of worry and self-loathing. He was not a weak man, but lately, all his feelings were right on the surface. He cried again, the same stale tears.

As he reached for a tissue, the telephone rang. The game was on. A man speaking thick Arabic mentioned Al Kubir, his Islamic Jihad story, and the doctor's revered name. He said to come to the marketplace at *Djemaa El Fna* tomorrow at two. The caller concluded with a threat, saying if he weren't there, there would not be a second chance. They would not contact him again. Dr. Mrabet's words came back to him. If it is the will of Allah.

After hanging up, he sat on the windowsill and smoked a cigarette, watching the soldiers man a barricade down the street from his hotel. Twice, he'd tried to go to the open-air market on the edge of the square four blocks away, but soldiers carrying machine guns had turned him back.

They told him it was not safe to be on the streets, to return home because a group of rowdies was shooting at anyone dumb enough to be out walking on the cobbled roads. Which was not true. Something else was going on in the city. Angry, he defied them to make a short jog across the road to a turbaned merchant who sold him a bag of nectarines, mangoes, figs, raisins, and a bottle of fermented palm wine.

Upon his return, the man at the desk told him he'd had two international calls while he was out. One from a woman with a husky voice who sounded like a man with a bad head cold and the other from a man with a high-pitched, nasal voice who asked if he was still alive and whether the hotel had been strafed by bullets during the afternoon ruckus. Neither person left a number to call back. He went upstairs and turned on the radio to listen to the evening program of foreign chatter and music.

That night, there was no show across the alleyway, though he did see the woman leave the building dressed in traditional, veiled garb. She walked with a man who wore European clothes and carrying two gift-wrapped boxes. They drove off in a small, dark sedan which had a jagged line of bullet holes in the door on its passenger side and a shattered rear window.

With the coming of dawn, he could see how dark and dismal the morning would be. It was not long before a strong wind whipped down the narrow corridors of the town, accompanied by forks of lightning and sheets of driving rain. Still, he heard military helicopters circling overhead, searching the streets for any odd activity. After breakfast, he went for a walk to see what was happening in the town.

To hell with the authorities. Maybe his press pass would carry some weight this time. Soldiers, tanks, and jeeps with mounted machine guns sat on every corner. Checkpoints were set up at all the key points of the areas where the trouble had broken out for the past four nights. Twice, he was stopped by police, questioned, and checked for identification. The fact that he was an American journalist brought scowls from the armed military men, but little else happened. He was allowed to go on his way.

Still, none of it was cool. He looked at his watch. He was screwed. It was well after three. If it weren't for bad luck, he wouldn't have any luck at all.

The Wasp

Before I got in here, my family had me locked up in a psychiatric ward for my safety. At least, that was what they said. Three times in Bellevue. How they caught me was when I went over to a girlfriend's apartment, and she ratted on me, called my sister, and told her that I was there. When I arrived, I had no idea she would snitch on me like that. I told her I was sleeping in all-night theaters, in hallways, in the bus terminal, on subways, anywhere but home.

He was out there, my husband. I was tired of being alone and hungry, but I feared him. He had beaten my ass so badly. The last time, he put me in the hospital. I was tired of being his doormat. I told her that. I was afraid for my life. He told me he would kill me. And he meant it, but it didn't do any good.

My mother, before she died, told me that I should have left him a long time ago, but I was too afraid to do it. He kept telling me that I wouldn't have made it without him. I was nothing without him. If I started a new life, he would find me, and I would be sorry I'd left him. He would make me pay.

"He's going to kill me," I told the cop, when I was at the police station to get the protection order. "He means it. He choked me under the water in the tub last night. I thought I was going to die. I don't want to die. I'm only twenty. I've haven't lived yet."

"What were you arguing over?" the cop asked. "Some man you were flirting with? I know how you young girls are. You see something you want, and you go after it."

I knew he was saying that because he had an audience. The other guys chuckled. Men stick together. A lot of them think all women are sluts and whores. I'm not like that.

"Yeah, what were you arguing over?" another cop asked me.

"I don't want a baby, and he does," I said. "I don't want to have a baby. I want to go back to school. I want to make something of myself. He's in a rush to have a kid, and I don't want to do it."

"Why not?" the first cop asked me. "Every woman wants to be a mother."

"Well, I don't want to be a mother," I said. "My mother had nine."

"Different fathers?" the cop asked with a smirk. A black woman had to have multiple fathers for her babies. Not one, but several.

"By three fathers. But that's not it. I'm just not ready."

The cop laughed with the other men. He was white, and so was the other guy who'd chimed in, but there were three black guys around the room too. It was a man thing. A woman should have babies, and that was that. You were put here on earth to be a breeder. I know that I was not put here to be a breeder. And I knew how hard my mother had it when all the men left. She was left to be a mother and a father to these kids, and it killed her.

"Is it about childbirth?" the first cop asked. He was trying to be nice, at least nicer than the other guys. "It hurts, but then you forget it. The pain goes away. My wife had five kids. You know, we're Irish. We like big families."

"And you're Catholic," the other guy teased. "The Pope doesn't like birth control."

"I'm not ready," I said. "I should have control over my body."

"Then you should not have gotten married," one of the black guys said.

"Are you a dyke?" another black cop asked. "You like women?"

"Hell no," I replied coldly. "I just don't want kids." I thought about other young women who pushed their baby carriages, proud to be mothers, female superior, proud to be breeders. They made you walk around them.

The first cop tried to lecture me about motherhood. "One day, you'll regret that you didn't have children. You'll be alone. Home, family, and the domestic life are all that matters, especially when you get old. You don't want to get old and miss out."

I'd heard about the biological clock, fertile time running out and menopause setting in. Tick, tick, tick.

I didn't think it was a disgrace not to want kids. I tried to make them understand.

"Do you like cats?" the second cop teased. He smirked, and the guys laughed.

"I hate cats," I answered. I didn't get it.

"But if your husband wants children, you should give him children," the first cop said.

"Being a mother is a part of marriage. Also, your parents would want to become grandparents," another cop said. "That's part of the cycle of life. Grandchildren continue the cycle of life, but you know that."

"My mother is dead," I said.

"I'm sorry," the first cop said. "You're not a feminist, are you?"

"No. I just don't want to have any kids."

The second cop laughed, though his expression was sullen. "You want to be a whole woman, right?"

"What's a whole woman?" I asked like he would know.

"Like biologically what you want to be, a woman and a mother," the cop said. "A whole woman. Normal. It isn't normal to be childless. It just isn't."

"It should be my choice, not his," I said firmly. "Can I get the protection order? If you don't give it to me, he says he will kill me."

Later, I moved out and tried to find a place to stay.

The rents were outrageous. I spent a couple of nights with a co-worker, but I had to move. She tried to feel me up. I didn't even know she was a lesbian. She had never tried anything before.

I rode the trains the following nights. I washed up in the station restrooms, changed clothes taken from the two shopping bags I carried and went to work.

The co-worker whispered to me, telling me she wouldn't do that again if I came back. No way was I going back. I was scared being on the streets, but I had no choice.

One afternoon, I walked into my boss's office. He was a computer nerd who loved science. Other nerds stood around, talking about some astronomers, saying they had detected water at the most distant point from Earth in a galaxy two-hundred-million light years away.

I waved to the boss to get his attention.

He waved me away. He was holding court and loving it. When

I tried to approach him in the hall, he chided me for being brazen and barging into his office. I just wanted to ask for a raise. Maybe my timing was off. Maybe just a couple of dollars an hour would have made finding a room in an SRO hotel a bit easier. All because I didn't want to be a mother.

I really didn't know I was being abused at first. I thought it was love, love between men and women, the routine matters of the heart. My husband had hit me, repeatedly. I didn't like it, but I put up with it. I'd look in the mirror, and my face would resemble a beaten boxer's face. Black eyes, bruised lips, twisted arms, aching limbs, and ribs. He stomped and kicked me too. I believed he hated women. I knew he hated his mother, but I think he hated females and women in general.

At parties, he'd loud-talk to his men friends with their girls. "See, she dances like a white girl. She dances like she fucks." He loved to shame me, embarrass me.

In bed, he laughed at me, said I had no rhythm.

My girlfriends said I should leave him before he killed me. The papers were full of guys who wanted to control their women, gave them low self-esteem, and shot or stabbed them. I couldn't leave him. I tried, but I couldn't. So, when I finally did, I just ran away. When it got hard, I started to make up reasons why I should go back. I always returned.

About three years ago, when I got off work, Jack, my husband, was waiting for me. I was headed to the bus terminal to get to my locker, so I could change clothes and wash up, but he dragged me to the car. He had a gun. I didn't argue with him.

"What is it you want from me?" he shouted. "You want a divorce?"

"No, I just want you to stop pressuring me about having a baby," I said, trembling. "I love you, Jack. I still love you. Give me time, please."

"We're married," Jack yelled. "I'm the man. I'm your husband."

"But you don't own me," I yelled in return. "I'm young. I want to live life. I want to go back to school and get a career. Is that so wrong?"

He poked me in the side with the gun. "Yes, it is if I say so."

"Why don't you want me to go back to school?" I tried to stay calm.

"Because I don't want them filling your head with all that nonsense," he said. "You don't need a career. I'm the man. I can provide for you and the kids. I can provide for this family. All you need to do is stay at home and take care of the kids."

"Suppose you leave the kids and me?" I asked, watching him start the car.

"I won't do that," he said, pulling out into traffic. "I love you. I just want you to do what I say. It's for the best. If your mother were around, she would agree. All she wanted was to have you happy. I'm a good husband."

"I want to do the school thing while I'm young," I said. "I can make you proud of me. You'll see. Then, we can earn money and give our babies a good home. I want a house in a good neighborhood. I'm tired of being poor."

We pulled up to a light. A cop car eased alongside us. My husband tucked the gun between his legs. He shot me a bitter glance, a warning to keep cool, and leaned forward to talk to the police officer in the next car.

"Do you know your turn signal on the left rear light is out?" the police officer asked my husband.

"No, I didn't, sir," Jack replied. "I'll get that fixed as soon as possible."

"You better," the cop said. "I'll let you off with a warning."

"Thank you, officer," my husband said, smiling.

The patrol car sped away. My husband didn't speak to me until we got home. He didn't ask me where I'd been. He acted like I had been at the job after a long day, but he didn't try to figure out what I'd been doing. My mother had warned me about him. She'd said he was a strange man. Maybe I should have paid her more mind.

My husband marched me down to a gynecologist, or "pussy doctor" as my mother used to call them so he could get me checked out. To see if everything was in working order. Jack was religious about doing the speculum bit every six months. No abnormal Pap smear for me. He found a woman doctor who was a friend of his mother's. Sometimes, he would sit in there as she asked me questions. I hated it. No privacy.

"Are you having any irregularities in your menstrual cycle?" Dr. Amado asked. "Bleeding heavier or lighter?"

"No." I loathed Jack sitting there.

"Do you examine your breasts for lumps?"

"Yes." I glanced at Jack, this two-hundred-and-thirty-pound muscle boy, weightlifting fool, watching me for any blemishes or flaws.

"Do you inspect your vulva for lesions, warts, or abnormal moles?"

"Yes."

"Do you examine your vaginal walls?" the doctor asked. "Is your discharge normal? Or is it indicative of a yeast infection?"

"Everything is normal down there," I replied.

"Take your clothes off and slip into the gown," she said. She chatted with my husband while I walked beyond the screen.

I returned and lay on the examining table.

She winked at my husband. Maybe they were lovers. She wasn't that old. She put on gloves, rubber ones, and took out the speculum. Cold metal.

"Watch again, and let me show you how it is done," Dr. Amado said, putting her hands on my body.

"With one hand on your belly and two fingers inside your vagina, feel your uterus, fallopian tubes, and ovaries. Are your hands washed?"

"Yes."

I hated my husband to see this. It was like watching me play with myself. I did as I was told, reluctantly.

"Now, with one finger in your vagina and another in your rectum, feel the area behind your uterus," the doctor said. "Good, that's it. Explore. Feel anything out of the ordinary?"

"No." I was ashamed. Totally humiliated.

"You might have a yeast infection, very slight," Dr. Amado said, holding up a glove to show me a thick, curd-like discharge. "I'm going to prescribe some Monistat. Do you get these often?"

"No, it's my first time."

"Is it VD?" my husband asked the doctor. "Has she been fooling around?"

"No, it's normal," the doctor answered. "Some women just get them. It will clear up. Also, drink cranberry juice and lots of fluids. Okay, Maya?"

"Yes, all right." I knew Jack would be interrogating me all night, to find out if there was another guy I was fooling around with.

Later, Jack was jovial in the car but upset at my angry face.

I was pouting, he said. He promised to slap me silly if I didn't lighten up. After all, he was my husband and not a stranger. I flinched when he raised his hand to slap me, and he stopped. He hugged me instead, cooing that he loved me, that he'd love me forever. He was a master of mixed signals.

In the beginning, Jack was the kindest man I knew. My family loved him. When he was just a boyfriend, he used to pick up groceries for my household, take my mother to the laundromat, drive us to church, even ride with her to the doctor's office. He was so patient, waiting around when she went to the drug store to get her medication. My mother had nine kids, but she was a lush, so the city took most of her young kids away. She couldn't take care of them.

And then she got liver cancer. The doctor told her she would get sick if she didn't stop drinking. She loved bourbon, straight up and drank like a fish. She hadn't started drinking until the last of her husbands had left her, and then she couldn't stop.

Yet, my mother had warned me about Jack. She'd seen through him. "Jack tries to act like butter wouldn't melt in his mouth, but I get a bad feeling about him," she said, just before she got sick. "He reminds me of Felix, my second husband. Something doesn't feel right about him. Don't marry him. Please don't, Maya."

I was stubborn. I wanted Jack.

When we got married, I wanted to stay with my mother because she was not well. He didn't want to live with her. We got a place in Brooklyn, in Brownsville. A dump where we gave parties, drinking and drugging. I got tired of that. He didn't want to leave the house. We got into a fight because I went to work as a secretary. I was always good at typing and stuff.

When we went out, he would always put me down, talking about my fat ass. "Man, she's definitely got a lot of junk in the trunk," Jack said, teasing me in front of the guys. "She's got a J-Lo ass, and she can fuck. I got to give it to her, she can tire a nigger out, but that's about all. She can't cook or do anything around the house."

He told me about he was screwing a co-worker, bragged about it.

One night, one of his crew told him he should respect me. "You shouldn't talk about how your lover swallows cum all night," he said to Jack, who'd probably only want to punch him out.

And jealous, oh man, was he jealous. Jack checked the car's gas gauge to see if I went where I should go. He monitored the phone bill to see if I made any calls to guys, itemizing it. He slowly isolated me, and I wasn't having it. I told my mother about it, and she said I should get out of there.

"He wants to control you," she'd said.

My sister, Inez, said I changed. I got quiet, shy, and meek. I never went anywhere except when Jack took me. I never went to family events, except for my mother's funeral and Christopher's baptism. He would snap his fingers like he would do a dog, and I would sit on his lap or in a chair near him. He would smack me in public or punch me, and I never thought about calling the police. I was scared to go against him.

"You don't know what he would do to me," I told my sister. "He's crazy."

One Easter, he beat me so bad I had to go to the hospital. He broke my jaw and busted a few of my ribs. The doctor who saw me never asked me about abuse, so I didn't volunteer anything about my husband doing this to me. He never brought up domestic violence, so I didn't either.

I went that spring, after the hospital visit, to a place where women went for counseling. A woman who knew my symptoms understood everything about me. We talked and cried together, but I would not leave him.

I took a long lunch with some co-workers. Had a few laughs and drinks. Jack was waiting for me when we left the restaurant. He hadn't said anything when he'd called that afternoon, and I'd said I was going. When he picked me up, he was all smiles until he pointed the gun at my heart and said I was a bitch.

"Who did you fuck?" he said.

"I don't know what you mean, baby," I said.

"I saw you with that man," Jack said. "I saw you with him."

"That was my boss. There were four other people there too," I quickly explained. "We were talking at lunch. We were celebrating a deal that came through."

"Are you fucking the bald, white guy?" Jack asked. "Is that the man?"

"He's my boss, damn it," I answered.

He slapped me across my face with the gun, hard enough to bust my lip and bloody my nose. I saw stars for a time.

He didn't say anything else until we got home. Then, he started yelling and screaming about how I was going to have his baby. It was time for him to claim what was his. A baby would announce what was his. Crazy talk like that. He blackened my eyes, and I had to take off the next day.

"You oughta thank me for not killing your black, whore ass," Jack said, holding the gun in my mouth. "You know that. You cunt bitch! You will have my baby, or I will kill you. That is final!"

I left him after that, a second time. I switched jobs. I cut off all ties with my family, my sisters, my brothers, my aunts, everyone. I got a new place. I got a new man.

I forgot all about Jack. I turned twenty.

Then, one day, I got off at my subway stop, on the number two train, and there he was.

Driving a red Honda, he wore a suit. He got out and leaned against the car. "Did you really think you could leave me that easy, bitch?" He held a gun to his side.

He knew where I lived, only two blocks from the train stop. I was screwed. I silently prayed and continued walking.

A day later, I got the protection order, one of fifty thousand the city courts grant every year. The judge said it would be the only thing I would need to start a new life. The maximum time for the order was a year. I figured I could use that time to put my life together. The catch was that I, as a battered woman, had to accompany the police officer when he served the order. Since Jack had moved, we had no choice but to serve it to him on his job.

The officer handed it to Jack, who was a salesman at a department store. He sold electronics, such as TVs and stuff.

I didn't want to go, but the cop said I would be safe.

A crowd of co-workers gathered around Jack as he was handed the order. The cop said the words and warned Jack not to come near me. A boss was standing near Jack.

"You got me fired, you bitch!" Jack shouted as I walked away. "You got me fired."

I knew that was not the last I would hear from Jack. I just knew it.

Three weeks passed. Daniel was my new man. Tall, thin, quiet, and almost serene. He looked like a basketball player, but he didn't play sports. He was a runner and ran in the marathons, the New York and Boston ones. He dressed very well, casual and classy. Always Bill Blass. I loved to drive his car, a vintage Thunderbird Sportster.

When it happened, I was in his arms and nude, like that first time. He held my heart within his cupped hands, showing me love like I'd never known with any other man. His kisses were soft and heated. I could dream with him of a future and possibilities, unlike the one I'd had with Jack where there was only darkness and hopelessness. I felt his dick inside me, the fire of it, the surging power of the hardened flesh. He took his time to drink in my scent and caress my sensitive nub, causing me to buck underneath him, easing him further inside until he flowed so sweetly and tenderly. Skin on skin. Sweating, touching, and writhing.

The funny thing was that Daniel never liked to sleep with me through the whole night. He kissed me on the lips and ran off to the shower.

I lay on the soiled covers, smelling the aroma of freshly-made love, and wondered why it was taking so long for Daniel to shower. I listened. No water, no splashing. The door was ajar. I tiptoed to the closet, grabbed my robe, reached for the gun in the top drawer. It was loaded. I opened the door and eased down the hallway until I pushed the bathroom door open.

"Oh, shit," I gasped. Daniel was sprawled on the tile floor, his hands up to his throat, a gaping hole in his neck. Blood poured from the wound with every beat of his heart. He tried to speak, tried to warn me, motioned with his limp arm toward something.

166

I turned and faced Jack.

His ugly face wore a distorted smile worthy of his deed. "If I can't have you, nobody will," he said. He held his gun at his side. "I told you that I'd kill you and anybody else that got in the way of our happiness. You will have my baby."

I shot him.

He fell against the wall, then pitched forward.

I shot him again, this time in the chest.

He slumped over with his gun hand lifted, and I kicked the gun out of his grasp and shot him one last time. The bullet went through his forehead.

I dialed 911 and asked for help. The operator put me on hold. Daniel was still alive, but barely. His eyes were glassy, and his hands were twitching. He was losing a lot of blood. He was going to die.

I went crazy that summer. They locked me up. I don't know how long. I was crazy as a motherfucker. Totally insane. I didn't do shit I was supposed to do. Early on in my imprisonment, I stuck my hand through a pane of glass. My mouthpiece tried to get me put in a minimum-security prison, but they decided on a place for the criminally insane.

One of the guards there tried to dry-hump me, thrusting himself on my leg and ass, like a dog in heat. I felt his dick. It was soft and limp against my butt.

This blondie made him leave me alone. This other sono-fabitch with him followed me all day. I kicked him in the balls, and he yelped like a scalded cat. Every time I tried to get some shut-eye, somebody fucked with me.

These folks were real nuts. One girl swallowed crushed glass.

Another chick jammed something jagged up in her pussy and bled to death. I caught the inmates having sex all the time with each other or with the guards.

When I told my sister, Inez, what was happening, she said nobody liked a tattletale. My other sister, Barbara, brought a couple of her church sisters to pray for me, made me hold a cross and read from the Old Testament.

"A woman is born of sin and trouble," Barbara said, pointing to my heart. "The Bible says that. Read the Old Testament. Remember Eve led Adam to sin. She ruined him. She turned him from God and all his glory."

"What are you saying, sis?" I asked.

"You killed him. A man," Barbara replied. "God will never forgive you. Killing is a cardinal sin. Didn't matter what he was doing to you. You should have left him. You don't kill him, for Heaven's sake. Now, look at you, locked up in here like some animal."

I remembered how Barbara was working as a clerk on a temp job about two years ago, just barely making ends meet, and her boss, a cracker, offered to give her a raise if she would let him feel her ass. If he could see her bare buttocks. And she let him. A woman is a sinner, yeah right. Damn hypocrite!

A year into my sentence, I was put in a straitjacket following a stunt I did. I tried to cut an assistant's throat with a jagged can top. They put me in a harness so I couldn't make any more mischief. That was when I made friends. Selma and Jan, both nut cases of the first order. Jan would tell the most outrageous lies imaginable. We would all listen to her and howl with laughter.

"When I was an actress, another actor brought in a soiled Kotex in a mayonnaise jar, saying it was used by Barbara Stanwyck," Jan laughed, cracking herself up. "Do you believe that?"

"No." Every woman patient on the ward screamed in glee.

"My father got drunk one night and called the FBI, saying he shot JFK," Jan continued. "My mother thought he was crazy. She left him after that with a deacon from the church. The old man went queer and ended up with a sex change in Soho. My brother said the last he saw of him was when he spotted him with a bunch of skinheads in the Village, wearing a red Mohawk."

Selma always laughed at her lies. She was a stout girl and had her tits bandaged up. I caught her leaning over, sniffing Jan in her crotch with a broad smile on her face. "You don't use it much," she said, sticking out her tongue coyly.

I was tied up for several hours of the day, my "agitation" hours as the hired help called them, and Selma and Jan took turns letting me smoke. They fed me cigarettes while they railed against men and their superior, arrogant sex. Selma said she was married once, had one girl, who was assaulted by her minister. The girl never recovered, lost her head, was doped up on meds and had a seizure and walked out in front of a bus downtown.

"I understand why you don't want to be a breeder," Selma said, her lips snarled. "To be honest, I wish I had never brought a child into this world. Men hate children. They hate babies. Men love sex, that's all. If we didn't have pussies, they wouldn't want to have anything to do with us. Think about it."

I wished I had kept my mouth shut.

Jan had the bright idea of collecting all the knockout meds

from her pals on the locked wards. When they had a cup full of them, they fed them to me until I lost consciousness and fell back on the bed. Millie told me all about it later; how Jan held the flashlight, so the girls could see, and how Keisha, another inmate, tied my arms down, and how Selma went to work with a needle and thread. Something about an African ritual or rite, closing the window of the body to the soul, Selma said to the girls.

When I awoke afterward, the pain was horrific. I howled in agony. The nurses and orderlies rushed into the room, saw the bright pool of blood soaked into the covers, and pulled them back. I writhed back and forth, out of my head with physical torment. It felt like a hot butter knife had been put between my bare thighs. One of the orderlies fainted, and two nurses carried him out.

"Oh, my god, how could anyone do this!" the head nurse yelled, pointing at my neatly shaved, stitched-up sex. "It's not funny. This is not funny at all."

Nobody was laughing, except me. The pain made me delirious, hysterical. Stitched up like a gaping wound. Neuter. A zero-woman reborn.

What it Takes to be Human

For the returning Veterans of the Iraqi and Afghanistan conflicts.

RECRUITING ABUSE

I was eighteen, and something was missing from my life. I was a good-looking, rawboned stud, just like my father. Girls thought I was cool. Shy, I didn't talk to people right off. Sometimes, I looked at my feet, lost in a world of my own.

My father suggested I go into the service because he didn't think I had the smarts to do anything else. He said the Army wouldn't mind if I was a little slow as long as I could shoot a gun. My mother got into the act, adding that the actor Lee Marvin was in the military long ago. I didn't know what I wanted to do. I couldn't have gone to a community college.

My father drove me down there and sat in the car until I got my papers. The people at the Army recruiting station didn't give a rat's ass if I was mentally slow, just like my father said. A guy next to me said he had a coke problem, but the soldier behind the desk offered him a job in the Army or Marines. Said they would work that poison out of him. It was the first time I ever heard about a war in Iraq and the whole slaughter on 9-11 in New York City. I didn't read the papers, use computers, or watch TV. The buildings came down in New York City in a heap, exploded by airplanes piloted by terrorists, and everything changed for good. Damn them Arabs!

Some of my family said the military would never take me. I scored a grade of thirty-three out of ninety-nine on the Army's entrance exam. My cousin said thirty-one was the lowest grade the military allowed for enlistment.

Off I went to basic training. There were few options in this economy, very few jobs, very few opportunities. Many of the young guys and gals from my neighborhood joined the service because the government always needed new bodies for wars halfway around the world. The recruiter kept saying I'd protect civilians on the home front by serving over there and keeping the Arab threat from appearing on our doorstep. I bought this line of bull. Bought it lock, stock, and barrel. I wanted to be liked. I wanted to serve my country.

UNCLE SAM'S A SURE BET

When I was on the rifle range, I thought even if I went to Iraq and got messed up, Uncle Sam would provide for me. One of the privates, a dude from the projects on Chicago's South Side, said the military had him sign a waiver because he was convicted of a felony as a kid. He'd carjacked an elderly couple, robbed them, beat the old man, and stole their car. We hit it off right away.

He said the military gave him an enlistment bonus of $20,000 and relaxed the rule that would have left him stateside because he had serious asthma. I heard other dudes got in the service even though they were overweight and autistic. Everybody got in these days. I wondered where my $20,000 went. Maybe my father had it. Funny he didn't say anything about any money. I knew what I was doing when I lifted my hand and swore to uphold the Constitution and the American flag. Most of the men in my family had joined the service, put on a uniform, and trotted off to fight a war somewhere, no questions asked.

WELCOME TO IRAQ

The people of Iraq were mad at us. At first, some of the vets said they welcomed us like liberators, like heroes. Tattered photos showed some of them pulling down a statue of Saddam in a town square someplace. But now, we had to be on constant look-out, ever watchful, weapons at the ready. The commander said never let more than a few of them gather in a crowd, or it could be our ass.

Sometimes, I was assigned to do rooftop observation. I used a special rifle with a scope on it so I could see things close. I looked at each door and each window, in the alleys, cars, and trucks, and I always watched the people walking or sitting along the street. Once, I saw some shady looking people on a roof, just shadows in the mid-day sun, and I lined up in my sights to get ready to fire. I sucked in my breath. Held it.

But when I looked closer, I saw it was a grandfather, gray-haired and stooped, playing ball with his small grandchildren. I had clicked off the safety on my weapon and almost lit them up. That would have been hell to pay.

THE GREAT SATAN

We were the Great Satan. We were infidels. Heathens.

We had to be careful when we traveled anywhere in Baghdad

or the provinces. Even in the gated communities of the government officials with private guards on patrol. We walked in the crowded Yarmouk market in the heart of Baghdad at our own risk.

Danger was everywhere: Tarmaya, Taji, Samarra, Ramadi, Fallujah, Kirkuk, Mosul, Tikrit, Rawak, or the Anbar Province. You could take a bullet anywhere and at any time. The only moments I really felt safe were when I was at the air-conditioned base some fifteen miles northeast of Baghdad, jiving with the fellas, policing the area, or going to get a bowl of chili at the Burger King they had there. Playing video games or lifting weights at the gym. Camp Victory.

Early morning, we went out in these convoys, a column of Humvees and tanks, with some Blackhawk helicopters overhead. The soldiers were sharp and salty, guns up, especially in open spaces and going past dark alleys. We had to worry about roadside bombs and snipers.

I used to keep two pictures inside my helmet—one of the former Black track star, Jesse Owens, to remind me to hightail it out of any of trouble. The other was of Grand Ayatollah Ali-Muhammad Sistani, the spiritual leader of the Shiites. Both served a purpose in saving my life. You used any advantage to save your life or those around you. You never left anything to chance or luck.

One day, in the convoy, we spotted a woman suicide bomber. She ran toward a group of soldiers and blew herself up, killing seven from my unit and injuring three. Maimed them real bad. This was the first injury I suffered in battle. A long, jagged slash along my thigh. It took no time for them to patch me up. Good as new.

War was not constant gunfire. There was boredom, waiting,

and then it would happen—ultimate terror. Shit-in-your-pants terror. It was either the dull tick of the clock or rapid bursts of bullets whistling around you, the adrenaline charging through your body, making you do foolish shit you would not do ordinarily.

A FUNERAL INTERLUDE

The Mitchells waited for their boys, my cousins, to come home. Both boys were in the Army, and Craig was coming home in a coffin to the base at Fort Riley, Kansas. They let me go home from basic training for four days so I could go to the funeral. We don't have many family members, so they made an exception. Craig had been killed by a sniper in Kirkuk just days before his wedding anniversary.

My other cousin, Gerald, a bachelor, had been seriously injured by friendly fire. Both cousins had wanted to make a career out of protecting their country. Boot camp. War. Whatever it took. Craig and Gerald, together always.

Craig's wife, Anna, was sullen, very distracted the last time I'd seen her. She'd wanted to get her hair done before seeing Craig off for the last time. PFC Craig Burke.

Only a year before he died, Craig had married his honey. He'd proposed to Anna during Easter church service, stammered the words of wedded bliss before the fact. He'd already asked her parents for her hand. He told them he wanted to live his life with her, have kids with her, then grow old with her.

At the funeral, Anna cried into her hands and didn't look at his casket. She whispered to me, her voice thick with tears, "He was everything to me."

I smelled a hint of whiskey on her breath. Her dead husband

175

had been a quiet guy, generous, friendly, and good-natured.

Gerald Burke, I knew him too and thought about him a lot that day. Gerald, sitting atop a tank, had hopped down to see a crowd gathered near a flower shop. A bomb blast took his legs off and left him with critical upper-body injuries. He was confined to a wheelchair and very depressed. He used to be quite an athlete. Track, baseball, and football. He was a letterman. Now he was all broken up. A mind of horrible memories. Nightmares. Especially when the Army doctors told him he had to undergo a series of complicated operations on his lower torso and arms.

Gerald pulled me aside at the funeral and talked to me like I was his child. He said, "I did all this for nothing. Look at me. Look at my brother. He's dead. Bush has to explain what he's done. He got us into a war for a grudge against Saddam. He's getting a lot of boys killed over there, needless death, needless suffering. He keeps telling us, the American people, this disinformation and tired slogans about victory and freedom."

I didn't believe his garbage. I believed in this country. I believed in America. I believed in Bush's words about not quitting the fight in Iraq. No cutting and running. No cowards. I believed in not giving al-Queda free rein in the Middle East. I believed in the fight against terror, Islam as a religion of madmen, and I believed in the strong defense of Israel. When Gerald said Bush denied the military what it needed, I didn't believe him. When he said the President put the military out there unprepared, short-changed the soldier's body armor, and got American troops stuck in a civil war without an exit strategy, I didn't believe him. He was lying, at least that's what I thought until going over there. Then, I saw he'd told the truth.

Sour grapes. Craig was dead, and Gerald was all fucked up. It was not America's fault.

Just before I went back to Iraq, Gerald was found dead in his hotel room by a maid. The weapon he used had fallen from his hand. He'd put his pistol into his mouth and pulled the trigger. Later, I learned the Army kept a long list of soldiers who killed themselves after their first tours or after they were wounded on the battlefields in Iraq and Afghanistan. I couldn't get the last desperate words Gerald said to me out of my mind.

PRESIDENT GEORGE W. BUSH

I started paying attention to our president. I watched him prance around the White House, pal around with Cheney and Rove, and dance various jigs and twirls. He loved being the bully. He loved being the sheriff from a B-movie. He loved hearing his own voice.

Bush: "If they stand up, step up, and with our help, we can accomplish the objective."

Bush: "I want the enemy to understand that they can't run us out of the Middle East, that they can't intimidate America."

Bush: "The most painful aspect of my Presidency has been knowing that good men and women have died in combat. I read about it every night. My heart breaks for a mother or father or husband or wife or son and daughter. It just does."

Connect all the dots. Radical Islamists. Iraqi politics in flux. Tribal chiefs. Iraq under Saddam's thumb for 24 years. Dots.

BACK IN IRAQ

On the Blackhawk helicopter, a Marine corporal tried to get my mind right. "These brave Iraqis take risks every day, trying to rebuild their country. We have these guys volunteering to be policemen or soldiers, knowing they can be killed at any time, and they show a degree of patriotism for their country that these lame bastards like Senate Democratic leader Harry Reid will never know. We're here to support the notion of a liberated Iraq."

I didn't say anything. I thought about Craig's death and Gerald's urgent pleas for help before he'd put a gun into his mouth.

The corporal continued, cradling his weapon and looking down at the war-torn city, "Fucking saying you're sorry will not bring the good troops we lost or those Iraqi civilians back. Apologies are not an answer. Their lives are on your conscience, on your soul. Their country is ruined. They live in absolute filth, sleeping on the streets, living in abandoned buildings, hungry, sick, and desperate. No lights. No water. Hell, Americans are so pampered, so soft. They never have to worry about being hungry, thirsty, or needing shelter. Another depression will do them good. Straighten them right out."

President Bush on the Voice of America radio show: "It's not a civil war because the government is still functioning, and we don't see an organization trying to overthrow it and assume control. We have several instances of sectarian violence that is trying to destabilize democracy."

The role of a soldier is to summon up courage and risk his life.

Iraqi security forces blown up or kidnapped or killed and corpses along the roads. Life as usual within the heavily fortified Green Zone.

An Italian soldier on his way south: "What is a democracy to an Arab? Can they truly appreciate it?"

In Haditha, eight Marines killed twenty-four Iraqis in an angry door-to-door sweep after one of our men was killed by a roadside bomb. The soldiers fucked the bastards up. They shot up six civilians inside a home following the firestorm of rage. Civilian deaths. Gunmen opened fire on shoppers and schoolchildren in Nasiriyah and Basra. The entrance to the car park leading to the hotel where journalists live was hit by two car bombs, and American soldiers and private security forces locked the area down. No traffic allowed to pass. Checkpoints.

Mortars and shots sounded in the distance, reminders of combat.

AMONG THE MUJAHIDEEN

The Commander striding through the men departing in another convoy: "Watch your ass, Take the fight to the enemy. Shoot with bad intentions. Kill everybody and everything in front of you."

I always associated bad intentions with my favorite fighter, Mike Tyson. The farther we traveled from the base, the more danger we experienced. Nobody had to remind me to bring my Kevlar helmet or my flak vest.

More and more, we saw bombings throughout northern and central Iraq. The bombers were sneaky about how many people they wanted to kill. They would time it just right to make sure the streets overflowed with pedestrians, cars, and buses. When we would get there, the first blast would have happened already, usually near a bus depot or a school. Minutes later, a pair of suicide bombers would attack in the same area, killing even more shoppers and onlookers. All we could do was to comfort the victims or put out the fires. Very cruel.

179

Another car bomber timed his blast to catch people coming out of a crowded mosque from prayers on the Muslim holy day. The Arab bomber parked his car in a largely Shiite area, where a market was situated across from the holy place. The terrorist in the car wore a police uniform. Army intelligence revealed that he'd come from Mosul, Iraq's third largest city, which had been rocked by violence and bloodshed. The bomb killed fifty-two and injured eighty-five people. A series of bombings happened during a two-week period while the military officials said everything was under control. Meanwhile, there was a collision between a school bus and a gas truck carrying a large number of explosives. The bombings in the Shiite area in Sadr City killed 144 people. The Sunni mayor of Baquba was kidnapped by fanatics and killed. Rough times.

I was on a security patrol with two plainclothes Iraqi men guarding a high-level Iraqi official, some deputy of Prime Minister al-Maliki, when suicide car bombers crashed into the motorcade, killing themselves and twenty others. Several people died on the street around the blasts. The car used by the bombers had just pulled out of a gas station blocks away from the explosions. The force of the bombs was very powerful. A metal bar went through the reinforced windshield of the deputy's car, impaling the official in the chest. He died at the scene.

President Bush on Armed Forces radio: "Listen, every war plan looks good on paper until you meet the enemy. This is a moment the Iraqis had a chance to fall apart, and they didn't. I understand war creates concerns. Nobody likes war. It creates a sense of uncertainty in the country."

JUST KIDS WITH BOMBS

The men captured a young boy with a highly-sensitive explosive belt taped around his waist. He mumbled his name was Jassem Ali. He was thirteen. A soldier tackled him before his finger could hit the switch that would have sent the belt into a murderous explosion. His older sister walked into an anniversary party and blew the hell out of herself, sending a ball of flames and a blast ripping through the dance hall, killing and wounding everyone within the sound of its roar.

Both bombers came from Iran and entered the city with fake passports. No one searched the girl, maybe sixteen, which was a grave mistake. The insurgents knew young girls and women were less likely to be searched, so they hid explosives under their clothes.

Some of the officials at the base said the terrorists who'd ordered these youngsters to blow themselves up gave them heroin and speed so they could face death with more courage. It's not easy to confront death.

Iraqi Prime Minister Nuri al-Maliki: "Iraqis are your allies in the war on terror. Iraq will not forget those who stood with her and continue to stand with her in times of need. We have gone from mass graves, torture chambers, and chemical weapons to the rule of law and human rights."

Maliki told President Bush that another U.S. military raid would never happen in Sadr City this year. Muqtada probably got to him and made him back off. Maliki sent a signal to Bush that he wasn't willing to cooperate with the U.S. against Muqtada, though he knew if the U.S. soldiers withdrew, that would be his ass. He doesn't want the U.S. to leave just yet. He wants to use the American military to keep control on the country, keep his pals in power, get the greenbacks and stockpile arms. Maliki is not a fool.

I couldn't forget Gerald's last words. The war was un-winnable. They'd chosen the wrong side. It was time to end the war. I'd bought into the American myth of democracy. I went there because of what the Arabs did to us on 9-11. I went there because of patriotism and freedom.

I went because President Bush told the bad guys to "bring it on." I went because Saddam, the King of the bad guys, was caught. I went because President Bush landed on an aircraft in a jet, with the sign "Mission Accomplished" that said the war was over. I went over there not knowing what I was getting into. I went over there thinking war would be easy because we were on the right side, on Democracy's side. I went over there, because God was on our side, on America's side, on the side where innocent lives were not snuffed out because some holy book said so.

WHAT WENT WRONG

On the day of my transformation, I accompanied a large convoy with three fuel trucks heading west from Baghdad to Fallujah. The Marines needed supplies and ammo. The military knew the convoy was risky, but it thought the trucks had a good chance of getting to their destination with a shield of eight armored Humvees, about a dozen heavily armed soldiers, and six Special Forces guys.

Under cover of darkness, we left the capital, hightailing it toward the embattled city which the Marines were desperately trying to hold against a determined enemy force. Somebody tipped the insurgents off because they were waiting for us. They knew our route, the equipment, the number of soldiers, and the exact amount of fuel we were taking. They had to or what happened couldn't have happened.

The convoy was attacked several times on the road. Their snipers had a field day trying to pick off our men, who returned fire at every sound, every shadow.

The military spokesman who told my family about the incident said there was a cluster of IEDs that exploded in rapid sequence along the side of the vehicles before the rocket attack on the first fuel truck. Our Humvee flipped over, crushing several guys. I saw a sudden flash. The driver of our Humvee slumped, and a bullet went through his left eye. Shards of glass and hot metal pierced flesh. The fuel truck caught fire, and some soldiers ran through the night, their bodies covered with burning oil. They ran in the open air like blazing torches. The blast knocked me off my feet. Slow motion, suspended in air. When I landed on the oil-slick ground, the left side of my face, my neck, my arms, and my hands were burned raw. Puncture wounds bled heavily around my scorched skin. Others could not get out of the flaming vehicles, deathtraps, sniper bullets raking over the doors in an odd rhythm.

Gunmen shot at the panicked soldiers who ran in zigzag patterns, knocking them down like backlit bowling pins. It was like a zombie movie where the lifeless forms would splinter into a spray of crimson and crumble to the ground. The smoke was black and thick. It was clear to me that I was on fire and missing parts of my body, screaming to holy hell that I was on fire, screaming for help. Flesh sagged off my bones. Flames licked, and low explosions rumbled. The men returned fire on the enemy on both sides on the street. I flopped around on the sandy soil, crawling until somebody dragged me to safety under a car.

A grunt yelled at me to stay awake, don't pass out. I thought if

I lost consciousness that I would die. That's what they wanted. They'd timed the attack to inflict the greatest harm. Our guy's dead bodies stacked up in pools of blood. Others blown to bits or burned beyond recognition. Like me. There was hand-to-hand combat on those trash-strewn streets that day while I screamed.

The whole block was almost leveled by bombs that left date palms and pomegranate trees in flames. Soldiers blackened and bloody from the blasts shot at anything moving and or still. People trapped inside collapsed buildings cried or screamed or tried to hide. Two Medevac birds flew in low. Apache helicopters attacking roofs and alleys. A huge blast tore apart bodies, ripped them up. Limbs, hands, and torsos disintegrated in a deadly instant.

A lieutenant glanced at my charred body, his eyes filled with shock. He covered his mouth and turned away, mumbling. I barely breathed, my face felt totally gone, disfigured and burned to the bone. Critical. My ears rang and filled with pressure.

"Medevac air, this is Eagle Six, ten KIA and three for chopper. Repeat. Three for chopper." The lieutenant yelled into the radio as I coughed and spat blood. PFC Barbecue.

We do this every day. The stench of death, piss, shit, blood, and cordite slammed into me before, and I blacked out before the bird left the bomb site.

A BALANCING ACT

Probably, the military should not have saved my life. Back in the day, soldiers were left to die if they were as hopelessly injured as I had been at that ambush. Forget the no man left behind bullshit.

They told me reinforcements arrived and really kicked the enemy's ass. House-to-house cowboy shit. About twenty minutes after I was wounded, they strapped me down for a helicopter ride to a hospital in Baghdad where the quick-thinking medics and technology kept me alive. The doctors told me later that I'd been flown to a hospital in Germany where the medical staff alerted my folks that I had suffered third and fourth-degree burns over fifty-five percent of my body. I endured more than twenty surgeries and had a foot transplant. Three fingers on my left hand had been burned to a nub. I was comatose for four months.

After stabilizing me medically, I was airlifted to Walter Reed Army Medical Center stateside, where I clung to life by a thread. They placed me in a deep coma to reduce the swelling of my brain while they attended the serious burns covering my body. They reconstructed my face or what was left of it. They glued my left eye back into the socket. When I woke up and saw my scarred mask for the first time, I realized the transformation forced on me by the war was complete. I was a hunk of charcoal that used to resemble a man, something that would never be tolerated by the normal public.

When they woke me up, the docs kept me on the move. The assistants moved me from ward fifty-eight, the neuroscience ward at Walter Reed, to ward fifty-seven, the long room where they sliced away damaged arms and legs of critically injured soldiers. Several doctors conferred with my parents about whether they should send me to The U.S. Army Institute of Surgical Research Burn Center in Brooke, Texas, near San Antonio. They wanted me close to home in the DC area.

Traumatized and feeling apart from my body, I had

flashbacks and nightmares. The sharp aroma of antiseptic, medicines, burn salves, alcohol, and bandages made it worse. Large splotches of raw flesh covered my head, neck, and torso. The docs said I was burned over most of my body and had a collapsed lung. My left arm was shattered and the other mangled. Lots of shrapnel peppered my back, stomach, and legs. I endured skin grafts, cleaning the burns, wash-outs, and surgeries where they grafted bone from hips to my arms and chest. I was put in the intensive care ward where they monitored me regularly.

I got three major infections. Doctors told my parents they might have to amputate both of my legs below the knees. Fast-clot bandages and coagulation powders, morphine, sedatives, and life support machines were my friends. The docs replaced part of my skull with a titanium plate. Headaches, anxiety, and depression followed. I spent eleven months at Walter Reed. Lots of paperwork. Traumatic brain injury. Post-traumatic stress disorder (PTSD).

A bit of disconnect, overwhelmed case managers, volunteers, and caregivers didn't make for an easy transition to civilization.

Stateside, the wounded soldiers got fine medical care, but the administrative part of treatment was lacking. Broken and emotionally wounded, soldiers tended to withdraw emotionally and stay in their rooms. In Vietnam, seven out of 100 soldiers injured in combat died. In Iraq, one out of 100 died. As a character said in a sword-and-sandal flick, the living would envy the dead.

THIS BODY

My parents, wearing sour frowns, were always by my side,

cheering me on. They explained my needs to the doctors, nurses, and other caregivers. They acted as my loyal advocates. I think they felt guilty about what happened to me over there. With my good eye through the bandages, I saw them crying, speechless and mournful at the sorry state of my health.

My father, his eyes puffy, kept saying he was sorry, so sorry, while my mother patted him gently on the back. They complained to me about the lack of caring and compassion all the way around. Even at Walter Reed, long delays due to massive caseloads were the norm. We never saw the same doctors twice. But saw plenty of mice and roaches. Lost medical files, indifferent nurses, patients lying in their waste. We saw it all. But I needed the care they gave me, so we kept quiet.

For a time, I couldn't speak. Had to write notes or do hand signals. When I recovered my speech, my voice came out slightly slurred. People had to lean over to hear me when I spoke.

Bush on vets: "We owe them all we can give them. Not only for when they're in harm's way, but when they come home to help them adjust if they have wounds or help them adjust after their time in service."

Finally, I was discharged with a huge supply of painkillers, sedatives, and a manual on the care of burns and wounds. I loved my doses of oxycodone. The street in my old neighborhood taped ribbons on the elm and maple trees lining the way to my home. The neighbors gave me a hero's welcome, clapping their hands and cheering as the stronger men lifted me in my wheelchair over the steps to the front porch.

Wrapped like a mummy, I settled into the basement apartment of my parents' home, feeling sorry for myself. Nobody cares what happens to us when we return. I knew that now.

Out of sight, out of mind. We fought the war, did our duty, and came back home, broken and crazy. Vets needed help, and the VA kept stalling and putting us on one list after the other.

"Can he speak?" one of my cousins asked my father, adding that I looked like Claude Rains from the movie *The Invisible Man* with my head and arms heavily bandaged.

"No." My father shoved me in the wheelchair into a corner of the room so I could see the hand signals from the people who came to see me.

An aunt hinted I could be crazy from the war, saying the docs weren't worried so much about the disfiguring burns on my face and body, but about the PTSD and chronic depression I now suffered from. My father chimed in on the subject, telling her thirty percent of returning vets from Iraq and Afghanistan had the damn thing. Like that meant it was okay.

"He can't do himself harm in the basement," he added. "And people won't know he's around if we keep him down here. We'll make sure he goes to the VA, but for the most part, we'll stash him down here. Best that way."

My little cousin used his fingers to try and pry the bandages from my head until Dad stopped him. "I wonder how he looks under there," he said. "He probably looks like a monster. Like Frankenstein."

That first weekend home, I awoke from a drugged stupor and found the windows covered with long, black garbage bags. I pointed to the windows, mumbling, asking for the reason for the camouflage.

"We blocked the windows because people were looking in them, trying to see you," my father explained. "I covered them, so they wouldn't gawk at you like a freak. Next thing, they'll start collecting admission to see the monster."

My family got into a habit of eating by themselves, not letting me join them, almost as if they were ashamed of looking at me. I ate alone. Many times, I overheard them discussing me as if they were hiding some cursed animal in their home, a mad dog on a leash, a disfigured beast foaming at the mouth that could contaminate anyone it came near. In those moments, I wanted to die. Once, my father left his gun near my bed, a hint of his feeling for my monstrous self, a suggestion that I would be better off dead. But I wanted to survive. Still, I left the gun there.

Some memories were pleasant. I had met a young woman, Janet, before I joined up. She was lovely, curvy, with long legs. She was the color of a freshly minted penny. She wanted out of this town at all costs. I promised her I would take her away after I finished up with my military responsibility. We went around for months before I signed up. The night before my departure, I gave her a ring and kissed her like I wasn't coming back.

"We're very close." Janet spoke tearfully to a reporter for our city newspaper upon my return. "By him coming home from Iraq as a war hero, it made me see him as other people do. It made us closer. In life, you know change will happen, but when it does, it can really shake you. We will manage to overcome this challenge. My sweetie loves life to the fullest, so we will get through this."

My parents, a private nurse, and Janet became my full-time caregivers. I relied on them to do everything for me. It was degrading, humiliating, and immoral.

When they propped me up in bed, my mother brought out one of the photo albums and showed me a photograph of a tall, athletic soldier standing in front of a tank in downtown

Baghdad. I teared up. I knew I would never look like that again.

My mother fed me some mush through a glass straw, a collection of nutrients and medication, to strengthen me. My father waited his turn to change the plastic bag collecting my waste. The shrapnel sent surges through my body, through my digestive tract, and left my insides a tangled mess.

I kept the gun by my bed.

If it Makes You Happy

"You're not so damn tough and probably not so bright either, big man."

The woman looked directly at him when she said it, her voice the sound of color—deep, dark-red. Fiery, suggestive, and full of passionate promises. Her voice, rich-toned and throaty, was the first thing he noticed about her, the thing he would always remember. Sexy, crimson hymns.

She wore handcuffs. Metal confined her wrists behind her back. She stood silhouetted against a high white wall while the guys from Hopewell Corrections Center tried to figure out how she'd managed to escape from her cell. She'd been missing for three days before a traffic cop spotted her coming out of a fast-food joint. She refused to tell anyone how she'd done it.

Now, she was being admitted to Newton Psychiatric Facility for observation. Her behavior was deemed erratic at the time of her capture, but he couldn't see it. She seemed calm and serene as she stood in custody.

What happened in the elevator going up to processing twisted his mind out of joint and started his obsession with her. With guards flanking her, she stood in front of him, her hands behind her, touching and caressing his genitals, stroking him until his legs almost buckled by the time the ancient elevator reached the seventh floor. She was something else, not your usual brand of woman.

"Don't forget me," she whispered to him, as they led her away, down the dimly lit corridor to the front desk.

And he didn't forget her. He fixated on her. A guard at the facility, he often saw her on the grounds, in the hall, or in the cafeteria. There were always people around her, usually men, laughing and talking loudly, so he had no access to this woman who was slowly driving him mad. He watched her eat, observing how her mouth with its large, soft lips worked and how her long tongue flicked at its corners. He watched her walk, admiring the smooth rolling of her wide hips and the inviting space between her thighs as she moved seductively among the other inmates.

Once, walking up the stairs in front of him, she stopped, backed into him, and did a quick bending twist of her ass into his crotch.

Oh, he was hooked. Totally and completely. Yet another black man bamboozled by lust and a hard-on.

"Don't forget me, sweetheart," she whispered.

An orderly, carrying a tray of meds, interrupted their chance meeting, standing watch until the couple exited the stairwell and went their separate ways. No fraternizing between staff and patients.

He never asked anyone her name, wanting to hear it first spoken from her lips, in that dark-red voice. The day before he tossed his life away because of lust, a vivid imagination, and a stiff libido, was the first time they really talked. They squeezed into a supply room among the shelves laden with towels, gowns, rubber gloves, and canisters of liquid soap. The woman pressed close to him, too close for comfort. Notions of taking her right there flooded his mind, already full of comparisons to a young, gorgeous Lena Horne—the post-vintage Cotton Club Lena, in full bloom. But everything had to be right. Exactly like he'd pictured it, over and over every night as he lay in bed and touched himself, thinking of her and that dark-red voice.

"I see you watching me, every day, all day," she said, her eyes locked on his. "You don't have to say what you want. I know what you want because I want it to. But everything comes with a price. Nothing is for free, not in this world."

"I hear that," he replied, thrusting one hand into a pocket to subdue his growing excitement. "What's your name?"

"You know it. Don't play dumb. I hate an ignorant man." She stepped back some.

"I really don't know it. I wanted to hear it from you."

That made her smile, her full soft lips parting like lush rose petals. "Amina. What's yours, Mister Man?"

"Terrance Stokes. My friends call me Terry. What is it you want? What is the price?" He moved within kissing range, pressing the heat of his flesh into her, his cheap uniform, a flimsy barrier.

"I want out," she hissed, the colored heat of her voice sparking her words, turning them into flames he felt burn through him. "You get me out, and you can have me any way you want. Nothing is too kinky or too freaky. Anything you want is yours, but you must get me out first. Once I'm back in the world, baby, I'm yours to do with as you please. How does that sound?"

"Hey, I'm no fool," he said, afraid to admit to himself that he even weighed such an offer. "How do I know you'll keep your end of the bargain? I'm risking everything here. My life will be fucked as soon as I break you out. It'll be over."

193

Amina laughed softly, the sound of it much like the tinkling of piano keys. She reached down, unzipped her hospital-issued pants, and inserted her fingers into herself. That got her squirming a bit, and she coated her digits with her juice, laughed again, and brought her fingers to his lips. She was tart yet sweet, like the taste of exotic fruit from an untamed tropical island.

She knew how to close a deal, playing on his dissatisfaction with his job and life, putting a spotlight on the collection of failures and disappointments that had hounded him since high school. He was a loser. But this would change things. It was a chance to tell the whole world—the entire planet, all the doubters, and bad-mouthers—to kiss his black ass. He was calling the shots in his life for once. Everybody would know his name, if only for a hot moment. His fifteen minutes of fame, coming right up.

Busting her out was not that hard. All it took was a few Benjamins for the guys at the main gate, more for the crew on the supply truck, several lies, and even more of both for the cat with the small plane that took them to the Texas border. The pilot, with his tiny Cessna egg beater that shook and fluttered with every breeze, was spooky with his endless talk of the ancient Aztecs and their knack for human sacrifices. He didn't want to hear that mess.

"Just get us to the border," he told the pilot.

When it was all done, he was tapped out, almost broke, with very little green in his reserves. He spent more bucks on cheap Tex-Mex grub and a rundown 1949 black Mercury Club Coupe. The fistful of Yankee dollars he slipped to the Mexican guards insured they were not stopped at the border or their suitcases searched. Another big break, with all the pharmaceuticals she was carrying.

"When do I get a chance to collect?" he asked, while they walked among the stalls of an open market, buying sombreros and sandals in a God-forsaken, unnamed Mexican village. "When do I get my night? I've done my part."

"Be patient." She laughed, showing very few teeth. "I gave you my word."

They crossed the street, walking into an area where gringos were rarely seen, especially black ones. He concluded that Amina was a beautiful pit bull with a mouthwatering body and vacant eyes, more *Hustler* than *Penthouse* and *Playboy.*

The town was essentially still except for the burst of activity at the market.

Walking together, they entered a battered hotel, its awning hanging by a couple of bolts, and went up to the desk where a somber man took their money and gave them a key.

"I'm beat, wore out," Amina mumbled. "I need some sleep. A few winks, and I'll be as good as new. Then, you'll get your big surprise, big man." She shed her clothes quickly and quietly, allowing him his first real look at her shapely brown body. It didn't seem to matter to her that he watched her so intently.

The heat was stifling, broiling, even for late October. He wondered if this was normal, if it was because of the diminished ozone layer or the abundance of satellites in the atmosphere. He lay on the bed, trying to cool off, his thoughts hot with worry and lust. What was he doing with this crazy woman? He knew some things about her, but not much of her troubled history, her dark fugue states, her loose grasp of reality. Her criminal file had been sealed, so much of the information he really needed to know was lost to him. Getting off the plane, she'd hinted she was a murderer but didn't elaborate on that criminal bombshell.

Before she went to sleep, she told him she forgot to bring her Thorazine when he'd broken her out of the state hospital back in St. Louis.

He laid on the bed beside her as she slept, their bodies clinging together with sensual dampness, close, in a spoon-like fashion. Outside, an old man wearing a frayed sombrero, leading a swaybacked mule packed with baskets of fruit, walked slowly across the square. His red-lidded eyes followed the man's wobbly steps until he disappeared.

Amina stirred in slumber, mumbled under her breath, then flopped her curvy brown leg over his. Gently, he took her tiny hand in his big one and kissed it, noticing the diagonal lacerations along her wrists, deep and multiple. Tributes to her madness. He felt a strange compulsion to lick her wounds, softly and lovingly. Instead, he moved closer and kissed her full on the lips.

She opened her hypnotic eyes, still vacant and unforgiving, and she did nothing while he tenderly planted kisses on her heart-shaped face.

"I think you're frightened of me," she said. "You know I killed somebody."

"But you explained that. You said it was an accident. You said he came at you wrong, and you had to cap him. Shot him before he raped you."

She worried her eyes with the heels of her hands. "Yeah right, forced vaginal entry. He wanted to pop the coochie. I told you that, but I left out some things."

"What did you leave out, Amina?" He couldn't afford to let her off the hook.

"Nothing I want to get into right now," she replied flatly.

Quietly, they rested on their sides, naked and sweating from the unnatural heat, pressing themselves against one another, full length. A total body hug that drove him over the edge, intoxicated by the nearness of her, her deep-red voice, and the touch of her soft, bronze skin. Sometimes, she kissed him, near his ear and on his neck, swift and popping kisses much like a boxer's jabs. He couldn't stand it, but nothing had gone exactly as he'd planned. The thought that he couldn't go back to his old, stale life lurked in the back of his mind, and then there was what she'd said. *But I left some things out.* What the hell did that mean?

He didn't want to think about whatever she hadn't told him, but that was not cool either. What you didn't know could kill you. This was their third day together. He needed to know.

Finally, with some coaxing, she talked. She told him about her family, then about herself and her hospitalizations. Once she began, there was no stopping her. She outlined her suicide attempts, told him how she'd slit both wrists, taken pills, and overdosed on drug cocktails. About the time she dove off a four-story balcony, her fall broken by bushes. She'd once walked in front of a car on the turnpike. Then, she recounted the things she heard and saw in her head.

"Paranoid, schizophrenic, slightly delusional, with psychotic thoughts. That's what they say," she said.

He listened, but nothing she said mattered. She was a beautiful black woman who had survived, was still standing despite everything. Maybe all she needed was a guy who loved her, really loved her.

"What are we going to do if you get sick again?" he asked, after the reality of her condition hit home. "We're on the run, and there ain't a doctor or hospital for miles. Who knows what kind of care you can get down here?"

"What are you saying?" she asked, gazing up at the ceiling.

He watched her hungrily as she stretched naked on the dingy-white sheets. Her breasts and nipples seemed swollen, ripe for seduction. His gaze roamed over her long neck, her slightly rounded stomach, and the triangle of black curly hair between her damp thighs. While she chatted away, he scooted down so he could put his lips on the dark aureoles of her breasts. Even from there, he could smell the exotic scent of her sex. One of his big hands barely concealed what her body was doing to him, getting hotter and hotter by the minute. His flesh hardened and throbbed, wanting to be inside her, if just for a moment.

"You know, with all this pressure and shit, anything can happen," he sputtered. "Hey, you haven't been out of lock-down that long, and you're not back to your real self yet. And we don't have any pills to cool you out if something happens. What about that other junk you got in your bag?"

She glared at him, her face morphing from a mask of concern to one of growing indifference. He'd touched a nerve, fingered an old emotional wound, and she was pissed off.

She got up in his face and jabbed a finger into his chest. "Don't come at me like that," she snarled. "I left with you. Don't disappoint me. I'm gonna have me some good times and real happiness. And if I can't find it with you, I'll go elsewhere."

I'll go elsewhere. That's what his wife had done years ago. He'd been here before. After that time when this honey from the facility, drunk at an office party, called his house and left a jive message on his answering machine. *It's yours if you want it, Terry.* His wife had intercepted the message, and it had almost cost him his marriage, then and there. She'd made him pay dearly for that one. Then, she'd gone elsewhere. For a time, they'd ventured outside their marriage with other lovers, looking for new carnal thrills. She only came back to him when one of her Romeos went berserk and whipped her ass. He took her back until the whole mess started up all over again. But none of that mattered now. Now, he was here, waiting to collect, waiting to get the rewards of a very special night. It'd better be worth it.

"Are we still cool?" she asked. "I need to know."

He was still somewhere in his head, mulling over the old terrain. He'd heard her question but didn't answer right away.

"Hey, Terry, are we still tight or what?" she asked, with teeth in her words. "You're taking too long to answer. Don't scare me, man. Don't get shaky on me now, not when I need you most."

"No problem, sweetheart," he replied halfheartedly. "It's all good. I'm in this to the limit, to the end. You and me."

Tears in her eyes, she leaned back on the bed. "Don't fuck this up. I'm counting on you."

Her short explosion of talk had altered the mood in the room and settled something between them. He looked at her, really looked at her, at Amina. Without the fog and haze of their situation blocking his view, he saw she was possibly one of the finest women he'd ever met. A real fox with bronze skin, curly, black hair, classic looks, a puffed mouth that guys would love to kiss, and the leggy body of a model with full, natural breasts. Not silicone. Not like his insecure ex-wife.

It was time to collect. Outside, the full golden moon rose in the dark-blue of the Mexican sky, creating an Aztec night with infinite possibilities.

Her hand on his rod broke him out of his thoughts. It sprang back to life, lengthening. He scooted back to her again, landing feather kisses on the soft base of her neck, on her eyelids, and down around her nipples. Slipping one nipple at a time into his mouth, he worked on them with consummate skill, all the while stroking her between her legs, teasing her clit with his thumb.

She seemed to relax, submitting to her body's urges, her eyes rolling back in her head as he trailed his tongue along the smooth flesh of her inner thigh and her stomach. When he traced his tongue in soft motion along the soft, meaty folds of her sex, she wiggled underneath him, her hips lifting off the bed. He parted her restless legs even more with his rough hands, his nose pressed against that precious slit, his mouth relentless against it.

Her moans increased in volume when he slipped expertly down into the wet, fragrant cleft between her legs, the pink snake in his mouth exploring the sensitive nerves inside her box, rotating and caressing her to new levels of desire, until she grabbed his head and held him hard and fast. After her moist body trembled a second and third time, she broke off his oral assault on her and told him it was her turn to please.

Slowly, she moved over him on all fours, her butt high in the air, stopping only when her face was mere inches from his dick. She gripped it at the base, squeezing the engorged flesh until it became this monstrous thing of a deep violet hue with thick veins crisscrossing its shaft. Giggling, she took him into her mouth, sucking and humming, her head bobbing as she bathed him with hot breath and tantalizing down-strokes. His legs quivered and bounced on the bed from the waves of pleasure rushing through his entire body. Her hands cupping his ass, she drove him deep into her throat, as if she was determined to swallow him whole.

"Easy, baby. Easy," he mumbled, feeling himself close to the brink. "Stand up and follow me. I don't want to get my knees scraped up."

She followed his lead and got up.

He watched her every sultry move. It was as if they were young lovers, unable to keep their hands off each other, sharing their first night of passion together. He cleared off the top of a wobbly wooden table against the far wall, knocking everything onto the floor.

He drew the curtains closed and motioned for her to come to him. "Kneel over the chair on the table."

She obeyed, turning her smooth, brown ass toward him. "Show it to me," he said before he entered her.

She did as he asked while he entertained ravishing, thug-ass thoughts of taking her long and strong. Passively, she showed it to him longer, reaching back to spread her glistening pinkness. He moved in behind her, breathing in short bursts, and entered her gently, grinding against her with purpose, hands gripping a finely-formed butt cheek. Each plunge was rapture. He accelerated his rhythm, picking up the pace as she arched up to meet his thrusts, her hands grasping the table.

"Tell me you love me," she said, in that deep-red voice. "Tell me, Terry."

He didn't want to appear soft, a wimp, so he said nothing. He kept busy, rolling his hips, pulsing inside her. She reared back, opened her legs wider, and let him slip even farther into her, into her sweetness. A hissing sound, much like an agitated cat's, came from her mouth. She wanted him. He gasped and gripped her shoulders as he urgently pumped into the back of her womb. She changed her tempo, rocking her plump ass against him in faster, wilder circles. They banged harder into one another, lunging in a crazy love dance, fucking with a maddening, animal passion he'd never experienced before. She dripped, wet on him to the base, tightening around him as she sensed every throbbing inch of him inside her.

"Say it, please," she pleaded. "Tell me you love me."

He finally conceded and said the magic words while she rode him as if she couldn't get enough. It had been a long time for them both, and for him, never like this. His dick filled her again and again to the hilt. He withdrew, and then pushed back inside. Her muffled shouts drove him to thrusts faster and harder, now moaning in harmony, as they rushed toward climax. Soon, she peaked, crying out her pleasure, overcome by the power of a clitoral explosion coupled with his continued pounding.

When the raging storm of desire subsided, she stared at him like she wanted to kill him. Her eyes burned into him, dark and brooding. Eventually, her mood seemed to pass, and she eased into his arms, laying still, mouth to mouth. It was evident that something had snapped inside her.

But I left some things out. That was the last thought he had before sleep seduced him.

A few hours later, they got a bite to eat—beef tacos, beans, and yellow rice, chased with three chilled bottles of Corona beer. She wanted to walk around town after the meal, although the sun was still strong and very few people were out. He relented and let her have her way.

On the outskirts of town, they rented horses from a wizened, old man who thought they were gringos, albeit *los Negroes* American, brought in to repair the roof of the ancient cathedral in town. They rode out into the flatland several miles away, following a dusty trail along the river, heading south. She laughed when his horse, a brown stallion, whinnied loudly from thirst and stopped to drink the grimy water. He stayed atop the animal, clutching the reins tightly, feeling its warmth and bulk beneath him. She dismounted and walked in front of her horse near the ragged sagebrush and cactus. For him, it was good hearing her laugh.

Eventually, they tied up the horses, took off their clothes and waded out into the river. The water went up to their necks, briefly cooling them. She swam closer to him, smiling, and put her arms around his neck. Her weight made him slip. He went under, the water going into his nose and mouth before he could resurface. They laughed and kissed after he got his breath back. He watched her swim out into the middle of the river with short, powerful strokes, the water shimmering as it rolled off her back and neck. Twice, she dived under the surface of the water, her exposed sex pointing up toward the heavens. He swam out to meet her, and they played like kids, swimming side by side, floating on their backs and splashing water on one another.

When the frolicking was over, they swam back to shore where she took a blanket from her animal and brought it to the riverbank. They sprawled on the blanket, ate the last of the dry tacos, shared the remaining warm beer, and cleaned sand from their toes.

She kissed him, closed her eyes, holding an arm over her face to shield it from the blazing sun. He lay there silently beside her, enjoying her company.

After a time, she moved closer to him, touching his face. "Baby, I left some things out."

"What?"

She said nothing else. Her full, soft mouth covered his, and her tongue slid between his lips.

203

Maybe leaving everything behind was not so bad. His ex-wife had never been this hot or spontaneous. With her, everything had been planned, thought out to dullness, according to schedule.

"The man I killed was my husband." Her voice was drab, lifeless. "He deserved to die. He wouldn't give me a divorce. I was in love with another man, and he knew it. He made my life hell. I only turned to someone else because he was such a mean bastard. My young lover left me too, walked out after I killed my husband for him. Something went haywire in my head. The doctors said I had a complete psychotic break, went totally nuts. Lost my mind completely. Do you hate me now? Do you still me love me?"

"Yes, I still love you," he stammered. But he had some doubts and fears.

"Does this change anything with us?"

"Not really." He examined her face carefully for obvious signs of madness and found none.

"I really am nuts, you know," she said brightly, taking his hand and sucking his fingers until he pulled away. His sap rose along with his dread of her.

Later, they made love all night, going at it in every variation possible, until they collapsed, exhausted, in the juice-soaked sheets, totally sated. He slept the sleep of the dead, as the saying goes. When he awoke, Amina was gone with all her belongings. Most of his remaining money was gone from his wallet. She'd left him chump change, a few dollars. Panicked, he raced down to the street to see if everything was gone, and yes, his precious black 1949 Mercury Club Coupe had been stolen too. His woman with the deep-red voice. Damn her!

While he stood, bare-chested in his shorts, a very pretty

Mexican woman with dark features and carrying a basket of white plastic skulls approached him, holding something. An envelope. She stood and watched him open it.

The letter consisted of five sentences, scribbled in childish handwriting. His hand trembled with anger as he read its painful black-widow message. *I still left some things out. I am crazy, and you could get hurt. I really like you. There have been others, before you, like you. This is the best way, for both of us.*

He stood, dumbfounded and completely confused like he had been slapped three or four times in the face with a blackjack. Or knifed in the heart. A real fool. He'd thrown everything away for one night of pleasure. His entire life, gone. Across the square, three people in skeleton outfits marched toward the empty market. A truck of mariachi musicians, fully dressed in their stage costumes, holding guitars, pulled up. The men jumped off and walked into the hotel. One of them held a large skull in his hand. Tomorrow was the start of the two-day Mexican Day of The Dead festival, the celebration of death and its many wonders. How appropriate for him right now, he thought.

Maybe he was crying a bit because the cute Mexican woman patted him softly on the shoulder and said, "*Mujeres, ellas dan mucha lata,*" which loosely meant, "Women can sometimes be a pain in the neck." True, but not in this case. Amina knew who she was and what she was about. He was the one who didn't know anything about himself. She'd done him a favor, walking away before she took his life too and added his scalp to the others. A real blessing, her gift of his life after that night of miracles. In his hands were a new start and fresh possibilities, Amina's gift.

All he could do now was wash up, eat, and take another

accounting of his few assets. There would be time to think about tomorrow and the day after that later.

A Crisis of Faith

It was one of the brightest days of fall. The sky was never bluer, nor had there ever been so many birds aloft, or grass so green and full. No one had alerted the family that he would be coming that afternoon, but the arrival of their reporters with TV cameras, trucks and notepads meant that something was about to happen. They camped out across the street from the small, brick house in tiny herds, huddling and talking as they looked up and down the road.

There it happened. The car containing him—their son, their brother, their uncle—came roaring down the street. The government-issue Ford was led by a single motorcycle cop and followed by another. If someone didn't know, they might assume it was a motorcade delivering a very important person, a political official or a show-business celebrity. But it was only New York State bringing him home. After fifteen long years in prison, Danny Poole was finally coming home after being unjustly jailed based solely on the unstable word of a young white woman.

When the car reached the front of the house, Danny remained seated while the policemen pushed back the horde of reporters who pressed against the vehicle. Slowly, he exited the car, no longer thin and no longer young. He limped toward the stairs, steadied by one of the patrolmen. His family burst from the front door, nearly bowling him over with hugs and kisses.

"Hey, baby! Welcome home, sweetheart," Alva, his mother, said, wrapping her thick arms so tightly around him that he could barely breathe. "We missed you so much. I knew those prison bars couldn't hold you. I just knew they couldn't."

He tugged at the collar of the cheap, black suit New York State had given him as a parting gift. The inexpensive fabric rode up his neck and legs. If anyone noticed that he looked older, his gaunt face more lined and wrinkled, they didn't mention it. Instead, the five close members of his family guided him in the house, mindful of his fragile appearance and apparent bewilderment at his sudden emergence into freedom.

His older sister, Irma, kissed him lightly on the cheek and looked into his ravaged face, a thinner carbon copy of hers.

"Danny, we're so happy you're home," his sister said. "We all knew you didn't belong there in the first place. We all knew that. Knew it then and know it now. When did they let you go, love?"

"Last night." His voice was a dry rasp. The words, his first, uttered in freedom. "But they kept me there until this morning. For processing or something." He sat on the well-worn couch in the living room, noting it appeared smaller than he remembered. His hand shook slightly from the nervousness that raced through him, surging and ebbing beyond his control.

He replayed the day of his arrest, the yelling and shoving of the station-house cops.

The young white woman had pointed at him and said tersely, "Yes, that's the nigger who raped me."

A large knot of tension grew in his stomach as he reflected on the bitter memory.

"Danny, Aunt Cece and Uncle Keith will be coming by later," his mother said. She smiled, brushing a bit of lint from her blue gingham dress. "We're planning a big party for you this weekend. Everybody will be here. Everybody."

He thought about everybody who had attended his trial and who had listened to the white woman talk quietly and earnestly about how he'd snuck up behind her, pinned her arms back, and held a knife to her throat.

"When I tried to shout for help, he told me if I said one more word, he'd kill me," she'd claimed. She detailed how he'd broken into her house, beaten her up, and forced her to "go down" on him.

Her pink, ruddy face with her thin lips and tear-streaked cheeks were stamped on his mind. What chance had he, a black man, had going up against the holy word of a violated white woman?

From the kitchen, his younger brother, Benny, came. Tall and proud, he bore a big platter of sandwiches—turkey and ham on wheat. He stood near the doorway, staring at Danny as if he were a ghost. A wide smile emerged by degrees on Benny's dark face, showing his deep joy and wonder at the return of the prodigal son to the fold. He stared at the abused, maligned son who had spent half his life behind bars for a crime he hadn't committed. All because he was black, and he didn't have an alibi for the night of the sexual assault. Fifteen years, fifteen wasted years. Time Danny could never get back.

Benny's smile faded, and his eyes showed concern. "Did they do anything to you in there?"

"Anything like what?" Danny didn't want to answer any questions about being inside—the endless battles between the strong and the weak, the bad food, the dank smells, the horrible feeling of being caged like an unruly beast.

"You know like...made you into a punk," Benny continued. "You're still all right?"

"Yes, I'm still a virgin if you must know." He grinned though his tone was harsh. It was the truth, but he could never tell them what it had cost him. He had almost killed two men up there. Had almost become a murderer. The brutality and the violence he was forced to commit to keep himself intact, to remain above the level of an amoeba on the prison food chain, was not something he wanted to talk about.

His brother and sister laughed and looked uneasy, relieved. His mother wore an expression that said she knew there was something he was not telling her, a truth that was not being spoken. She pointed to the press photographers climbing over the front porch, tramping all over the grass and flowerbeds, aiming their cameras through the picture window, flashbulbs popping with blinding regularity. Where was the right of privacy for his family?

Benny walked to the window and pulled the curtains shut dramatically, using both hands.

Danny clapped, bringing giggles from his sister.

"Lawd, why don't those people leave us alone?" his mother cried, rolling her eyes. "You know they won't have nothing good to say. All looking for new dirt."

He flashed back to the white woman's face during the trial and remembered the string of her bold lies, certain to send him to jail. "He was so huge. I mean big and tall." Her voice quivered with each syllable. "It was not enough for the nigger, with his animal smell, to take me against my will, but he sat there afterward and smoked two cigarettes, chatting with me like I was his girlfriend or something. He wouldn't let me wash up, take a shower. I felt so dirty and unclean. Ask any woman who has been raped. She will know what I mean. And he's a nigger. In the old days, he would have been strung up without all of this fanfare and expense to the taxpayers." That was what she had said, right on the witness stand. The judge let her say it.

"Are you bitter, son, for what they did to you?" his mother asked, holding the plate of sandwiches before him.

"How would you feel if someone took all those years from your life?" he replied, his body stiffening. "Took them and you knew all along you'd done nothing wrong. Knew you were innocent and nobody believed you."

"We believed you, Danny," his sister said quickly.

He couldn't look at them. None of them believed him. The truth was that his family had believed the white woman, just like everybody else had. How could justice be real for anyone when all a person, especially a white person, had to do was point a finger and yell that an innocent man was guilty?

Much of the evidence that could have freed him was never introduced at the trial. Even his own court-appointed lawyer had advised him it didn't look good for him, that his only option was to plead guilty to aggravated sexual assault, take the lesser charge, and put himself at the mercy of the court. Which he had done.

The past fifteen years had been a nightmare from start to finish, with the cards stacked against him from the moment he was arrested outside this very house. The cops hadn't believed a word he'd said, even the fact that he lived on this block until they checked it out.

When he saw the composite drawing of the suspect, it looked nothing like him, but to the cops, it was a Rembrandt.

Perfect. They'd claimed they had evidence linking him to a series of rapes in the swanky neighborhood, petite white women ravished by a big Mandingo buck who pounded on them afterward. The lead detective, the man who testified, said he never had any doubt of Danny's guilt, not after the woman was able to describe him in full detail.

Danny shook his head to clear the painful memory.

"You were a Christian before you went in there," his mother said. "I know that's what kept you from becoming like the rest of them. That undying faith in Jesus. I know you must have leaned on him when it seemed like there was no hope. Right, Danny?"

"God doesn't visit prison, Mama," he retorted. Like many men on the inside, his faith was a private thing, a flame he held deep inside, not something he proclaimed to the world. Then, and now, it was nobody's business but his own.

"Don't blaspheme in this house, child," his mother snapped. "I didn't raise you like that. I raised you to have some respect for God and the church. I won't tolerate that under this roof. I don't care what they did to you in there. You won't bring that mess in here." She shook with righteous indignation.

He stood rigidly to signal an end to the conversation, heading stiffly toward the kitchen, where the comforting smells of fried chicken, collards, cornbread, and black-eyed peas wrapped themselves around him like a warm, winter coat, taking the chill out of his heart, whispering to him of the times when Daddy had been with them, and the word family had meant something.

Until the moment Daddy had suffered a heart attack and dropped dead in the kitchen, near the ice box, his family had been a cocoon of safety and protection.

The door sounded, and the loud, raucous shouts of Uncle Keith and Aunt Cece echoed throughout the house like gunshots. Uncle Keith, pale-skinned and rail thin, was all dressed in the latest Mack Daddy chic. Aunt Cece, big as a Goodyear blimp, was made up like a tart, dressed in colors that glowed in the dark. They were known throughout the entire clan as the most uncouth, uncivilized members of their bloodline, capable of turning out weddings with their antics, skilled at ruining family dinners with their tasteless comments. Heathens, his mother called them.

"Where's the jailbird?" Aunt Cece screamed at the top of her lungs. "Come on out and let us look at you, boy. Come and give your favorite aunt a hug."

Uncle Keith chortled, his Adam's apple bobbing on the downbeat. "You can run, but you can't hide. I won't bite you, son."

Danny eased out of the sanctuary of the kitchen, walking unsteadily toward the intruders, his arms at his sides. This was the last thing he needed on his first day of freedom. Why couldn't they come tomorrow when he was gone?

Both had spread the worst lies against him during the trial, giving the cops all manner of gossip against him, even leading them to the mother of a girl who'd once accused him of him slapping her around. Her boyfriend had done the damage, but Danny had been an easy target, the perfect fall guy. The police had taken him in, but nothing had come of that false accusation because it happened when he was under eighteen, a juvie. Those records were supposedly sealed. Supposedly. His heart hardened at the remembering, and his arms remained glued to his sides.

"It's a damn circus out there," Uncle Keith said, looking

out the window. "The press is all over the place. Cameras, the whole nine yards, even Channel Seven. I talked to the tall, brown-skinned girl from Channel Four and told her I was like a father to you, Danny. That you were pretty much a good kid, who got a bad break. 'But you got to keep a close eye on him,' I told her."

"Why did you say something like that?" Danny glared at his uncle. "I'm trying to start a new life, and you go and say some stupid shit like that. What are you trying to do to me?"

"Danny, I'm like your father, now that he's gone," his uncle said. "I know you better than anybody. You forget I knew you when you didn't know how to flush a toilet."

"Keith, nobody knows him better than I do," his mother said, moving between the two men. "I'm his mother. Don't forget that. I know my own boy."

Aunt Cece gently elbowed his mother aside, stretched out her arms, and enveloped him inside them. He was trapped for several minutes, choking on her powerful White Orchid perfume and baby powder.

His uncle peeled Cece away. "Honey, that's enough. I don't want this boy getting any bad ideas. You know, it's been a long time since he's been with a real woman."

Aunt Cece laughed, but no one else did. For once, his family, his close kin, were behind him. That made him feel a little better.

"They had that white girl on the news when they said they was letting you out," Aunt Cece reported. "She said she was happy for you, that the court would not let you out if you were guilty. Said it still made her nervous and scared to see you outside of prison, said it was just a mistake, that color had nothing to do with it. Said she was saddened by it, but she wasn't going to beat herself up over it. Said she was going on with her life."

"Enough, Cee," his mother snapped. "Can't you find something else to talk about? He doesn't want to hear any more about that foolishness, especially about that cracker girl. She ruined his life."

"Just why did they let you out, anyway, Danny?" Aunt Cece asked, acting as if she hadn't heard one word the older woman said. "I don't get it. They found a hair strand and arrested some other black man. How does that work?"

"Danny didn't do it," Benny snarled. "They had the wrong man."

"RNA, right?" his uncle said, proud that he knew the scientific term.

"DNA," Danny snarled, walking away from them. "Are the bedrooms still in the same place? I need to lay down. My head hurts."

The doorbell rang again. It was another reporter and camera crew, asking for a few words from the family for the nightly news. Just something about how it felt to have Danny home, about how the law had finally come through for them, how they felt about the $20,000 check New York State had offered for the time he'd spent behind bars. Danny kept walking while Uncle Keith happily filled in the blanks for the reporter.

Wearily, Danny entered his old bedroom, looking at the small bed, the beat-up desk, and the stacks of boxes in one corner. Nothing had been touched since the night of his arrest. He grinned at the familiar sights and smell. He was home. He had survived everything—the beatings by the guards and the other cons, the shank attacks, the bad food. Nothing had trampled his spirit. Nothing.

There were times when Danny had had to hide his spirit to save it, times when his faith was repeatedly tested. He'd had many moments of doubt, even more of despair, but he somehow managed to hold to a spark of belief that God would eventually right the injustice that had destroyed so much of his life.

He hadn't become a fervent religious mouthpiece as many of the men in prison had, sprouting their newfound beliefs with an almost separate passion. For many years, he'd even stopped praying and gave up talking to God altogether. While he sometimes thought that it would be better not to believe in a Higher Power, Danny knew that hidden spark of faith enabled him to survive, so he wrapped it in a cloak of cynicism to keep it burning safely deep within. But no matter how bleak his future looked or how hopeless he felt, even in those moments when Danny feared that perhaps God had given up on him, written him off, and tossed him away, he couldn't bring himself to give up on God.

Feeling the tentative warmth of the spark growing into something greater, Danny sank to his knees on the floor of his childhood room and offered a prayer of sincere thanks. His eyes fluttered, but he kept them shut. That was the always the hardest part of praying for him—not the words, but keeping his eyes closed.

"Yea, though I walk through the valley of the shadow of death, I will fear no evil for thou art with me," he said, not opening his eyes even when he felt another presence in the room with him. Kneeling beside him. Praying along with him.

He recognized the raw, husky voice of Aunt Cece, saying the words of the familiar verse right along with him. They finished on the same note. She struggled to her feet with his help, pinched his cheek, and quietly left the room. But before her departure, she put a finger to her lips. He understood; this was their secret. Their private piece of serenity and joy.

After she left, Danny was numb. Nothing was as it seemed. She was more than just a loud-mouthed hellion, an uncouth harpy, but a woman who had a devout sense of faith and belief in the Almighty. Faith, that word again. In that instant, he realized what had helped him to survive all those years, in the darkest moments of his transformation from being an average hardworking man to a caged animal.

He sat on the bed, stunned by his epiphany, and with trembling hands, took out a cigarette. It took him almost five minutes to light it. Yes, faith, the evidence of things unseen yet believed. He could now acknowledge it. His divine faith like that which had sustained all his kind from the slave ships to the boardroom and beyond. Not just grit, determination, or spunk. But faith. Or something like that.

About Robert Fleming

Robert Fleming, a freelance journalist and reviewer, formerly worked as an award-winning reporter for the *New York Daily News*, earning several honors including a New York Press Club award and a Revson Fellowship. His articles have appeared in publications including *Essence*, *Black Enterprise*, *U.S. News & World Report*, *Omni*, *The Washington Post*, *Publishers Weekly*, and *The New York Times*. His non-fiction books include *Rescuing A Neighborhood: The Bedford-Stuyvesant Volunteer Ambulance Corps*, *The Success of Caroline Jones, Inc.*, *The Wisdom of the Elders*, *The African American Writer's Handbook*, *Free Jazz*, *Rasta*, *Babylon*, *Jamming: The Music and Culture of Roots Reggae*. His fiction titles include *Fever in The Blood*, *Havoc After Dark*, *Gift of Faith*, *Gift of Truth*, and *Gift of Revelation*. He edited the popular anthologies *After Hours* and *Intimacy*. He has taught journalism, literacy, and film writing at Columbia University, Marist College, City University of New York, and The New School.

Thank You

My editors are awesome, but they're human. If you found a mistake in the book, please let them know by sending an email to info@fullsailpublishing.com so they can fix it.

If you'd like to connect with me, I'm on Facebook and always up for a chat about the blues, books, writing, and life.

With love and gratitude,
   Robert